The
Pirate Queen

Charlie Hill

Stairwell Books //

Published by Stairwell Books
161 Lowther Street
York, YO31 7LZ

www.stairwellbooks.co.uk
@stairwellbooks

The Pirate Queen © 2022 Charlie Hill and Stairwell Books

This is a work of fiction. Names, characters, businesses, places, events, locales, and incidents are either the products of the author's imagination or used in a fictitious manner. Any resemblance to actual persons, living or dead, or actual events is purely coincidental.

ISBN: 978-1-913432-58-4
p14
Cover design: Rose Drew
Thank you to Edinburgh University for the image of Gráinne meeting Elizabeth

Also by Charlie Hill

The Space Between Things
Books
Stuff
I Don't Want to go to the Taj Mahal

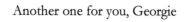

Another one for you, Georgie

Monday 5th September, 1650 – Castleburke Estate, Balintober, County Mayo

It is Maude's tenth birthday and Catherine sets off early from her cottage. A light rain is falling as she walks up the hill to the new house. The cloud is low and the estate is heavy with dew. Despite the drizzle the views of the house – three stories high, handsome in grey stone – are as imposing as Theobald intended. Not that Catherine dwells on this, not today. She is early for the morning's Latin and early too for her usual breakfast with Patrick, but this does not concern her either because today she has other things on her mind. She slips on the muddy path up the hill, hurries on, righting herself with the thought of what the hours ahead might bring.

Patrick is in the entrance hall. He is remonstrating with the housekeeper about the firewood they are burning; it is alder instead of oak and this will never do. Catherine shakes her head. Dear Patrick: there is something reassuring about his predictability. Seeing her, Patrick dismisses the housekeeper with a wave of his hand and smiles at his friend. 'You're early today!'

'I am! I thought it would make a change.'

'What's the occasion?'

'It's Maude.'

'Of course. Her birthday.'

'And I've had an idea. About how I can help her.'

'Her studies aren't going well?'

'On the contrary. She knows enough Latin to start on the Summa, and her embroidery is coming along. But I am worried about her. She is solemn. Her brightness is still shrouded in something like grief – incomprehension perhaps, or too much comprehension. She is untethered too. She has been since…'

'…So what do you have in mind?'

'A little something to help her regain her spirit,' says Catherine. 'I don't know if it will work, but I'm going to give it a try.'

'Her spirit you say? I'd like to talk to you about that actually. Theobald has plans of his own in that regard. Come on, let's get something to eat.'

They pass through the dining hall to the kitchen. There is no-one at work yet and Patrick spreads two slices of bread with butter, fetches pickled anchovies from the pantry. Catherine thanks him and asks – as she often does – if he'll try some. He declines with a theatrical shudder and they sit at the table and eat.

'So,' says Catherine, 'what are Theobald's plans?'

Patrick pauses. 'He's worried. The future of the estate is in doubt.'

'Is there a storm coming in?'

'Always.'

They both smile, but Catherine notices Patrick's doesn't last.

'What is it this time?'

'Oh this and that. But it's serious. We stand to lose it all this time. Every last thing.'

'What is it? Ireton? Cromwell?'

'Yes. And no. It's more complicated than that.'

'Please Patrick, don't you start.'

'But it is. I mean Ireton's Roundheads may yet take Limerick, but that does not concern us. What I'm talking about is retribution for

2

our part in the rebellion. They intend to make us pay in land. Those of us too weak to resist, in any case.'

Catherine dips her bread in vinegar, the fish long gone. The intrigue sounds familiar. Scarcely a week passes without Theobald hosting gatherings of powerful men, or at least men with the trappings of power. Each day is a new chaos of rumour and ferment and at the heart of it are the pretenders who seek him out to parley and plan for war or its avoidance. He has welcomed noblemen from the King, Bishops from the Church, representatives of the Confederacy in Kilkenny; men like James Tuchet, competent enough but bloodless too (at least until the sack appeared and he took to hunting bats) or Malachias O'Queely, almost Machiavellian in his cunning. *Almost* Machiavellian. Catherine winces as she recalls the story of his delusional machinations and the dismal brutality of his end at the hands of Scottish mercenaries. Then there was the Nuncio Rinuccini – replete with entourage and finery – come to stir the pot from Rome. All things considered, the roster has not been a promising one – so much brocade, so little wit! – and it is no surprise that the chaos is ongoing. Catherine understands then. 'But what has it to do with Maude?'

Patrick tilts his head, looks at her askance. 'We need to make new alliances. Theobald has arranged a meeting. With John Browne of the Neale. It is taking place at Rockfleet on Wednesday. We are setting off this afternoon.'

'Rockfleet?'

'You remember Rockfleet Castle? I'm sure I've told you about Rockfleet Castle.'

'Of course, of course. But does he not usually host such gatherings here?'

'He does. But like I said, this is different. He has decided that Rockfleet's associations will serve him well in the matters under discussion. Give him an advantage, throw his guests off balance. Whether or not he is right in this judgement is not for you or I to question. It is certainly true that if he is to succeed, he needs all the heft he can muster.'

'Again, I understand. But why does he need Maude there? And me?'

'It's nothing to worry about.' Patrick stands, passes a crust of buttered bread to Catherine. 'Anyway. It is good that you are early today. I needed to have this talk with you and I have a lot to do.'

'As do I,' says Catherine. 'I have to go and prepare the library.' She smiles. 'I still haven't got used to saying that!'

'That's what I mean when I say we stand to lose it all. I mean *everything*. Remember that.'

Catherine nods, but she is unconvinced. She is interested in politics, in the choreography and masquerades of vengeful men – she is alive! how can she not be? – but she has little time for it today. It seems unlikely, however bad the situation is, that Theobald will lose everything. He may be more vulnerable than some of his peers, but he is a Lord and a Member of the Irish Parliament and such positions count for something. And besides. Today Catherine has her own business to attend to. As she watches Patrick leave the kitchen, this is what occupies her mind. She doesn't know what Theobald wants of her and Maude but whatever it is the castle will be the ideal backdrop for what she has planned.

After the morning's Latin, Catherine sits with Maude in the library and wishes her a happy birthday. Maude is unconvinced.

'Did you have gifts?'

'A Bible,' says Maude, 'from my father. The Douay Rhiems. It has gold leaf on the cover.'

'That sounds beautiful. Do you like it?'

Maude shrugs. 'I don't understand it very well.'

4

'We can look at it together next time,' says Catherine. She regards Maude keenly. 'Maude? Have you been told we're going away today?'

Maude's eyes brighten with a flash of something that, although more than likely mere enquiry, cheers Catherine. 'Really? Where to?'

'The sea.' Catherine tries to give the word an emphasis that Maude will be unable to resist.

'Oh.'

'I think you'll enjoy it.'

'I don't know. I've been before. Why are we going?'

'Ah. Now that *I* don't know. But the air will do you good.'

'I don't want to go.'

'What *do* you want?' says Catherine, and although she means to sound kind she doesn't, and regrets her choice of words. Maude doesn't answer. She looks at the floor and then out of the small window, at rain. Catherine sees that she is near tears, that her light is dimming once again. It is suddenly very hot in the room – the kitchen must have started work – and Catherine is helpless in the face of the little girl's despond.

They set off for Rockfleet Castle after lunch, in a column both impressive and threadbare. At its head ride Theobald in full regalia – a plumed Cavalier hat, chest plate and thigh length Spanish boots – and Patrick. Behind them, Theobald's teenaged son Miles – similarly attired and uncomfortable in the saddle – and the bearer of the Viscount's standard. Next are half a dozen foot soldiers dressed for business, their helmets glinting in the wet; two carry pikes and there are four with muskets. Then comes a stagecoach, new but unsuited to the track, which slurs joltingly through the sandy mud; two wagons carrying cooks and craftsmen, wood and kitchen supplies and tents for the retinue; and lastly, limbs splayed as they slip and slide, a muttering gaggle of labourers and porters and maids.

Catherine and Maude are in the coach. It is dry at least, though this is little consolation when they are thrown from their seats. Maude seems put upon and does not speak. Catherine is contemplating how best to introduce her idea to her charge, but she is distracted; as the coach slews, she looks out at the detail of the passing countryside and is transported by her feelings of nervous anticipation to the memory of an earlier journey, and to her first exposure to the lands west of the Shannon.

It was three years ago now. Catherine, twenty-two years old, was living in Dublin. 'Come to Castleburke,' Theobald had suggested, 'and teach my daughters.' They were talking in The Stationer's Company, a shop managed by Catherine's father; Theobald had been thumbing the latest print of *Foras Feasa ar Éirinn* and Catherine had indulged him in conversation. She was educated but not a teacher and had barely heard of Mayo, yet she agreed to the proposal with scant consideration. Many times over the course of those three trying years she thought back to that decision.

Because Catherine was born to Dublin. For as long as she could remember she had immersed herself in its manifold charms, the challenge of its filth and dazzle. She walked streets that reeked of fish and human waste, on her way to the orchard at Piphoe's Park, where she read plays from her father's shop under laden trees and enjoyed the opining of her contentious peers; she had been euphoric in the gloomy wash of the street lights – whoever could conceive of such a thing! – and shocked by the pity of the city's crumbling walls. Then there was the theatre on Werbergh Street. That had been a common haunt. The place was run by a serious minded young man called John Ogilby, who was known to her father. Most of the performances were considered unsuitable for a young girl but Catherine was not to be denied and spent many hours enthralled by Shirley's *Constant Maid* or Burnell's *Landgartha*; on occasion she was allowed backstage or to tread the boards in an empty house she imagined filled with an audience for her own work. The theatre was a short lived enterprise – it closed when Catherine was just sixteen, a casualty of the rebellion – but by then Dublin was in her bones.

Yet life in the city had its disadvantages too. Foremost amongst these was a lack of free rein. Her father was kind-hearted and encouraged her reading and her interest in Werbergh Street, but Catherine knew if she stayed in the city she was tied fast to The Stationer's Company and this was not enough. Catherine was ambitious and even if hers was a nebulous want, its presence was no less demanding for that. There were other constraints. Although she was a confident woman, Catherine could not move about the place unaccompanied – instead she was allocated a chaperone, the wife of a friend of her father's. Catherine questioned why. It was true there were dangers in the streets of the city, but the woman's near constant presence was more a sop to propriety; she was employed to safeguard Catherine's virtue and Catherine resented this and failed on many counts to see the need.

Her decision to take the role in Mayo then might have been a whim – Catherine knew she could be inconstant – but there had been sense there too, for as much as she loved the city she was keen to sample something new. Perhaps some time beyond the Pale would provide her with a unique stimulation? A greater freedom? Something new, the chance to live a little differently? Perhaps the need to fit into the moulds of men would lessen and Catherine would be able to abandon herself to an adventure of her own making? It was certainly a possibility. 'Connacht is different,' her friends told her, their eyes alight with excitement and alarm, and although she paused to question the evidence on which they had based this judgement, there was an irresistibility to its logic.

Her father was unconvinced. 'I forbid you,' he said.

'Oh father. We have spoken about that.'

'Very well. Then I would rather you reconsidered your decision.'

'I understand.'

They travelled to Mayo together. Although Catherine didn't ride well, they went by horse. It took days. They crossed the Shannon at Snámh Dá Éan and before long her hopes were struggling like their horses through the cold wet earth. Because Catherine's friends had been right in their surmisings. Connacht *was* different. It might have been a different country so far removed was it from the life she had known. Connacht was wild and dark – a deep and ancient dark, a dark both clamorous and hushed – and without the obvious refinement and sophistication of the city. They passed through villages called Annaghdown and Ballinrobe and Kinturk. They stayed in lodgings where they were served curd pancakes, from which Catherine, though game, recoiled. There were abbeys and ruins of abbeys through which howled winds with more intent than even those of the coast back home. There were castles. There was evidence too of the rebellion that had caused so much anxiety in Dublin just six short years before: forts and fortified houses pock-marked by musket fire, disquieting people, harrowed and hollowed-out by war: on the road they saw men with muskets, men on horseback with lances, they saw Scottish fighters armed with long swords and small round shields, mercenaries abandoned by their old paymasters and waiting for their new; they passed brown-robed monks and sisters in black habits; there were townspeople who stood and stared at Catherine's suede gloves and riding dress – was that envy? mistrust? or disdain? – and she felt alien and unwanted in their eyes.

The most disturbing encounter took place in a town called Tuam. Catherine and her father were watering their horses when they were greeted by a farmer herding sheep. Her father asked how far it was to Castleburke and the man's friendly demeanour changed. He demanded to know their business there and when informed that they were to meet with Viscount Mayo, he hurried off without reply. After that Catherine had to remind herself with each passing mile that the journey had been her choice and that it should be considered more of a challenge than a trial.

This trip is not as long nor unbalancing as the one she took then, but there are similarities. The short distance to the coast takes them through a threatening landscape – under mountains, through villages that are little more than a sinking of huts into the mud of the hillside, through peat bogs – and the sense of expectation is stimulating. Rockfleet is somewhere Catherine has wanted to come for two years. She has heard so much about the place that it is a home of sorts away from the privations of the estate, a part of her imagination that she visits when she needs to indulge herself or feel whole.

And now she is here. She arrives as the sun is setting across what must be Clew Bay. Maude's mood has not improved but Catherine is wide-eyed, all questions of Theobald's motivations forgotten. So full is her imagination of the stories she has heard of this place, that she is taken somewhat aback by her first sight of the castle itself. It is not what she had pictured. It is starker, more austere. Less grand. Less grand? It isn't grand at all. It is a stone tower, isolated save for a row of tiny cottages, that seems to rise out of a bog.

But then there is the Atlantic. Around two sides of Rockfleet Castle curls a body of water that flows widely out to the bay and the sea. And even from a rain-misted distance, the ocean is a formidable presence that inspires awe and quiets for a moment the exhilarations in Catherine's head.

Later, Catherine visits Maude in her quarters on the third floor. Maude is sitting in a chair by the fireplace, in which burns nourishing oak from Brackloon. Maude's embroidery is in her lap but she is not working at it; instead she stares into the flames. She is surprised to see Catherine. 'What are you doing here?'

'I've come to see you. I think you are suffering. And I have something that might be a balm.'

Maude looks at Catherine, sees nothing in her hands. 'It's not another teaching of the Summa is it? I am enjoying it, really I am, and it gives me much to think about, but I am tired.'

Catherine laughs. 'No, dear Maude, it is not more Latin. Rather I had a mind to tell you a story.'

'I don't understand. An entertainment? To raise my spirits.'

'I suppose it might be regarded as such. But more too, I hope.'

Maude is puzzled. Catherine fetches another chair from the corner of the room and pulls it close to the little girl's. Together, they watch the fire. Catherine is nervous – wary of Maude's delicate state – but she is excited too. She knows the stories she will tell will have their gaps and untruths but she has heard enough to know that this is the nature of stories. And besides. At least in her telling they will be her gaps and her untruths, and then in time the gaps and untruths of Maude.

She begins…

'So now Maude, I'm going to tell you a story. Some of the language of the story may be unfamiliar to you but please bear with me, for when I first heard it, it was new to me too. The Western vernacular of the Gaelic tongue is musical but it can be impenetrable to those more used to Leinster Irish.

The story is about a woman in the world of men. Her name was Gráinne Ni Mháille or Grace O'Malley and it is no exaggeration to say she bested all the men who crossed her.

Gráinne was the mother of your father's father. That's right – you have in your heart and veins the blood of a legendary woman! And Gráinne was legendary. She was the Pirate Queen, Gráinne the Bald, Gráinne Mhaol, the Sea Queen of Connacht, the Dark Lady of Doona; she was a woman of such infamous and defiant renown that an English knight who would have hung her from the highest gallows said she was 'the most notorious woman on all the western coasts, a traitress and the nurse of all rebellions in the province for forty years.' Gráinne lived in Rockfleet Castle and a dozen castles besides, in Kinturk and on Clare Island, at Cahernamart and Kildavnet, at Doona, Belclare and Bunowen. She ruled the lands of Murrisk and she also claimed the sea, touring the waters out of Clew Bay in ships that gleamed and cut the waves like dolphins. She was a wise and judicious woman, a woman courageous and determined and terrifying in equal measure and it is a sin against her name that her story is not better known and shared more often than the stories of lesser men.

Gráinne's story began, like yours, with a little girl who felt lost, as though she did not understand her place in the world. Like you – and I dear Maude – her mother passed when she was young. About her, as is often the custom of these stories, nothing is known. Gráinne's father however, was a man of land and power, like your father, the Viscount of all Mayo. His name was Eoghan Dubhdara Ó Máille, the Black Oak O'Malley – and he was Chieftain of great and resourceful clan. The O'Malleys claimed they were 'powerful on land and sea' and none gainsaid it. The O'Malleys were herdsmen. Their lands were green and rich. They kept the finest Dexters alongside Draft and Hobby horses and long-legged sheep from Tipperary; they were fishermen and sailors and traders and their waters stretched from Erris Head to Inishbofin.

Eoghan took the herring and cod he fished to Spain and the wool and leather from his livestock to the land of Magellan and the great Flanders city of Antwerp, where he exchanged fish for wine from Jerez, met with lords and merchants from across the seas and brought back muskets and Japanese porcelain, sugar and spices and silk. In this way he amassed a fortune in both wealth and power that was unsurpassed in all the lands west of the Shannon.

Although she was born to the name Ó Máille, Gráinne was never marked for the adventure of her father's trade. Her clan lived like all in Mayo by the ancient Brehon Law and Brehon Law decreed that a woman was of lesser bearing than a man and provided for in property alone. Irish Laws and English Laws are of common aim in this regard, with man at the centre, like Galileo's sun. And so it was Eoghan's son Donal who would come to the title Chieftain and all that came with it, and he who, from an early age, was advised in the ways of a leader of men, taught by household kern the ways of the rising out, the use of bow and dart and sword. Gráinne, meanwhile, was instead prepared for the life of a wife and mother, for it was in such roles that her value lay. So she was taught Latin and French and embroidery – as you are too! – and was groomed like a Spanish Barb. But this was not enough for the little girl who would become a queen.'

Maude frowns. Catherine pauses. There is a lot for Maude to absorb; is she expecting too much of the little girl? 'You are not finding this too taxing a story?'

Maude's frown deepens. She regards Catherine with an admonishing glare. 'It is a simple enough tale. I am concentrating, that is all.'

'I am pleased!' says Catherine. 'Because Gráinne was moved by the world, as I have seen you to be.

She looked upon each dawn with eyes that grew wider than an open thistle and felt in her heart a stirring she could scarce contain. And as she watched her half-brother grow to manhood she was filled with a determination to replace him in the eyes of their father, not for reasons of envy but rather a desire to explore the possibilities of his duty over hers, to carve for herself a place of worth in this otherwise dispiriting world. This was not an unreasonable ambition. If Donal showed promise in matters of war, if he shot and fought with blades and rode and hunted boar as if to his position born, he held no enthusiasm for the unfathomable Atlantic wherein lay much Ó Máille power. Gráinne, on the other hand, had always been captivated by the sea.

Did you see the sea, Maude? When we arrived this afternoon? Was it how you remembered it? Because the sea is a beast of ceaseless change and Gráinne, well Gráinne loved it. She loved its roars and whispers, its shifting depths and surfaces, the way it held both fables and the future within its waters; she was unbound by its dark and shimmering possibilities. She taught herself to dive like a gannet and swim like a marlin and once she disappeared – not into the woods, like a certain young lady I could mention – but beyond rocks, when the tide was highest. This was not wise but Gráinne had no care: she returned to her father with three baskets of the finest dulce. Late in the evening, when fires were lit and bards held court, she would press her ear to her father's door and hear of voyages to faraway lands, of purses of doubloons and bales of silk and cutthroat pirates and English dogs. She longed to avail herself of this perilous allure and promised herself that when the time was right she would take ownership of the seas that were so intimately bound with the fortunes of her family, and in doing so prove her suitability for the role for which she had – by virtue of the traditions of men – been overlooked.

One day, while her father was planning a trip to Cadiz, Gráinne requested that she too be allowed to make the journey. She was a young girl at the time, not much older than you are now. Her father's response was to give his daughter short shrift, for it was not acceptable for Gráinne's sex to be at sea. But Gráinne was not to be deterred and demanded to know the reason why. Eoghan was bemused by her persistence and attempted to deflect her with talk of her value as the daughter of a Chieftain. 'You are to be married,' he said, 'to secure influence for the Ui Mháille, and no man will take as a wife one already wedded to another. For this reason, however much you love the ocean, I will not encourage your passion and you cannot sail with me.' Still Gráinne inveigled. 'There may be men in Cadiz to whom I could be profitably betrothed. Why not let me present myself, a catch as fine as the fish you take to sell?' At this Eoghan was forced to resort to more obvious methods of dissuasion and forbade his daughter on the grounds of her appearance – 'For your long hair will surely entangle with the rigging' – at which point Gráinne tired of the exchange. That very day she cut her hair short like a boy and clothed herself in breeches and demanded of her father 'Will you take me now?' Eoghan had no choice, and Gráinne sailed with him to Spain.

The sometime rambunctious crew were unsure how to treat the shaven-headed girl. She was young and vulnerable but a force of nature also, like a gusting wind; not to mention the daughter of their lord and master. They were wary then but Gráinne was more calculating than she was callow. She sat with them and ate with them and demanded they teach her Mack and Maw; she beat them at chess and saw to it they were beguiled. Once in Spain she charmed the merchants with whom her father had come to trade and was presented with pajamas of silk, a leather purse from Cordoba and the lasting admiration of The Black Oak O'Malley. From the moment of that voyage, the shorn chief's daughter rejoiced in the nickname Gráinne Mhaol or Gráinne the Bald.'

At this, Maude breaks into a smile; not a smirk but an expression of joy. It is the first such look that Catherine has seen in weeks. The room is now deep in shadow – the fire only glows and it is nearly time to light a candle – but Maude looks unlikely to sleep any time soon and Catherine, warmed and made hopeful by her reaction, continues.

'Despite her father's best intentions then, Gráinne's affair with the sea endured. The trip to Cadiz made her more determined still to fulfil her ambition and as she grew older her voyages became more frequent. She sailed with her eyes and ears open, observing the workings and absorbing the rituals of her family's gallies. She went with Eoghan to France and Portugal and learnt with every passing hour how to change course and cajole the oarsmen, read the wind and navigate the open sea, how to negotiate the sandbanks and uniquely treacherous currents of Clew Bay. She became a sailor the equal of any O'Malley man, and was accepted by sailors who had never hitherto considered putting to sea with her sex. As more as words of her deeds spread her influence throughout the clan, so Eoghan began to view his daughter as he might a son.

Alas, Gráinne was not at liberty to imagine that she might be treated like a man. Even as she demanded her father's approval, she had to tread the path prepared for her. And so it was that at sixteen she was married, by arrangement of the chieftains of the Ó Máille clan, to Dónal Ó Flaithbheartaigh, Bright Prince of Iarthar Chonnachta and Tánaiste to the

Clan O'Flaherty. The union was made with an alliance in mind – the O'Flaherty's were the ruling family of Ballinahinch and it made sense that they should be tied in marriage to the Ui Mháille of Murrisk – and as soon as they were married, the couple moved to Donal's Bunowen Castle. The arrangement was a success. Gráinne's standing with her father and her prowess as a sailor ensured her importance to the deal transcended that of a mere chattel and the families shared sovereignty over twice the land and twice the sea that they had once enjoyed. But for Gráinne there was another pleasing aspect to the union. For all that men and women have their duty to perform there are few that can resist the call of amorous companionship. And so it came to pass that Donal and Gráinne fell in love.

Before long she and Donal had exchanged gifts that spoke of such a love. Donal presented Gráinne with a glove of lamb's skin, dyed red, after the gauntlet on his crest, and Gráinne gave Donal a silken pane of St Brigid, stitched in blackwork by her hand. For years thereafter they lived contentedly, as man and wife on land and sea. Donal herded horses and raised cattle – they had a thousand head of Dexter between them – and Gráinne taxed the fishermen who sailed in Galway Bay. Between them they owned many acres of land on which grew wheat and barley enough to feed all the lands west of the Shannon. They enjoyed hunting and racing horses – yes! she was a better rider than I am! – and watching the sun set over Aillebrack Lough. In the evenings they played cards and drank oat beer and Gráinne soothed Donal with the harp; she taught him poetry by Tuileagna Ó Maoil Chonaire, Connacht's most splendoured prince of words and in the summer the two of them walked on the slopes of Binn Ghuaire and Donal repaid her in kind, telling stories of the lands they surveyed, of Barnaderg Bay and Ballynakill

Harbour, of Inishbofin and Inishark. Within five years, Gráinne had borne her husband three children, Eoghan, Méadhbh and Murchadh and they too brought the couple joy. But Gráinne's experience of happiness was destined to be fleeting; like a flower that blossoms each year from the cold hard earth, she would shortly have to prove herself anew.

Not that we will learn more of this tonight. The story of your Gráinne is too rich to be taken in gulps and swigs – rather it is to be sipped and rolled about the tongue. We shall continue with it tomorrow.'

And Catherine finds herself standing and curtsying, with a flourish, before a startled and enraptured Maude.

Tuesday, Rockfleet Castle, County Mayo

Catherine wakes in the castle. It is an odd feeling and for a moment she is disorientated, so she runs her fingers along the grain of the wood of the bed, lets the soles of her feet feel the cold stone of the floor, moves to the window. The rain has closed in overnight and obscures Clew Bay and the grey sky helps to ground her once more: she is in Mayo; she is in the castle of Gráinne Ni Mháille.

Leaving her quarters she goes downstairs to the kitchen and is assailed by a tumult. Rockfleet is getting ready to welcome guests and the trappings of nobility are being given centre stage. She sees boxes of porcelain and forks and cases of wine, old tallow candles being replaced with those made of beeswax; in the kitchen one cook prepares a porpoise and another encases a goose in mud. Catherine takes a deep breath – she has never understood the attraction of porpoise – and asks the hard-pressed cooks for some eggs.

The eggs arrive with bread and butter, and she gulps them down with relish. When she has finished she seeks out Patrick and, seeing him in the entrance hall engaged in earnest discussion with Theobald, waits. Theobald finishes and walks away.

'Can I ask you a question?'

'If you're quick.' Patrick has sentries to organise and is distracted, looking this way and that at men carrying axes and planks of wood.

'I would like you to arrange passage to Clare Island. I would like to visit the abbey. The one you told me about.'

'Clare Island? That's a fair distance.'

'Really? Are we not on the bay?'

'We are. But things are not always as simple as you imagine them to be. The easiest crossing is from Kilgeever Abbey, which is – at the speed you ride – a good hour away at least. Can I ask why you want to go?'

'I would like to take Maude. I think it will do her good.'

Now Patrick gives her his attention, frowns. 'I'll have to check with Theobald. Our guest arrives today.'

'But you said we weren't needed until tomorrow.'

'That's as maybe. Even so. He may not approve.'

'What harm can it cause?'

'You need to be careful.'

'Is there a storm coming in?'

'I'm not joking. Theobald is under a lot of pressure at the moment.' He pauses. 'Maude is very important to him.'

'As she is to me, Patrick. Please?'

Catherine's 'please' is born, in part, of confusion. Everything about her friend's usually phlegmatic demeanour is ruffled. She knows he can be blunt, and sometimes his wit is dry, but if she had to characterise his manner of speech today she would call it alarmed. He took pride in choosing his words with care. So what did he mean by saying Maude was 'very important' to Theobald? By questioning her intent with regard to the little girl? Catherine cannot tell if he is genuinely impatient with her for some reason, or struggling with the arrangements for the visit, or both. She almost asks him, decides against it.

'Very well,' says Patrick and Catherine is grateful. He is in conflict, but he is a good friend. And it is important his reservations do not interfere with Maude's revival.

Catherine makes sure Maude is wrapped in a cloak, then they set off. Patrick has secured for Catherine a small and biddable horse and Maude sits behind, holding on to the saddle. Ahead of them rides Conall, one of Theobald's most trusted men. Maude is talkative. She asks 'how far away is Spain?' and 'how long did Gráinne live in Rockfleet castle?' and 'what happened to Gráinne's brother?' and then 'did Gráinne do battle with men?' Catherine is delighted by Maude's enthusiasm and struggles to recall the purpose of her plan: was it to provide succour? Or distraction? Either way, it brings to mind her own introduction to Gráinne.

When Catherine had arrived in Mayo, it seemed a lawless place. There was a malign busy-ness to it, a sense of menace that buzzed like horseflies in her ear. At Castleburke she was frequently unnerved by the sound of panicked messengers announcing their arrival in the middle of night; once, shortly after making her new home, she had been woken by the sound of a musket in the early hours of the morning. She was later assured it had been discharged in error, but even so, she could not help but wonder if she had made a terrible mistake in leaving Dublin. Ever determined, she tried to alleviate her sense of isolation by striking up conversation with the maids of the estate, the wives of the grooms and cooks, whose cottages neighboured hers. But as friendly as they were, the people here were poor and more, there was a benighted aspect to their existence: they were uneducated and unread and spoke little English. They offered Catherine little solace. It was only Patrick who provided the relief she had sought.

Had she been desperate? As much as she disliked the notion, perhaps she had. It was true she longed for the more familiar unpredictability of Dublin, but she also missed the companionship of her father. Either way, when she had let it slip to Patrick that she was lonely, he had responded like the generous-spirited man he was.

From then on, the two of them would snatch the odd half an hour during the day and walk together and he would tell her about the plants and birds and animals that had contributed – as a woman accustomed to the streets of the city – to her feeling of dislocation. He told her about willow trees – 'the bark will kill all pain' – and foxgloves – 'take the juice of twelve leaves and it will cure the fairy stroke'. They saw sundew, prolific in moss and he pointed out bunches of herb robert and yellow flag and birds with thin rasping cries that wheezed from the grass; at the sound of a lapwing Catherine remembered he grinned like a child. Catherine was enthralled by his knowledge and by his language too: her Irish was rudimentary, and here was Patrick conversing in English yet talking of traonach, invoking draiocht and describing sceitimíní.

Then there were the stories. In the evening, when their work was done, they would drink buttermilk and sometimes wine and sit in front of a fire, and he would tell her folk tales of the King Guiare and his bard Seanchan, of Meadhbh the Queen of Connacht and of Fionnabhair her daughter, stories unlike those Catherine knew from books and from the stage, more immediate somehow, sadder and more beautiful. There was something about his tone that suggested Patrick intended them to be cautionary tales but Catherine was more inspired than disconcerted.

The richest and most involving of the stories Patrick told were those of Grace O'Malley – Gráinne Ni Mháille – a woman who lived on the lands of Mayo and called them her own. The stories unfolded in great rushes of pride and anger and passion, in snippets of insight and pith; sometimes Patrick seemed unsure of the particulars but his delivery was compelling and the storytelling was like an incantation and it became the background to Catherine's new routine, its rhythm, its pulse. And for all that the people, and the hillsides, and the bogs and the mountains of these worlds – of her new home – were foreign, Catherine began somehow to feel like

21

she belonged, connected as if by spider's silk or the love of God to something at once less distinct but greater than her ken.

And this was not the end of it. On the day he finished the story of the Pirate Queen, Patrick presented Catherine with a knife. It had been a gift to his grandmother. She had worked for Gráinne Ni Mháille who had passed it to her one day, in thanks for her service. It was a simple enough weapon, long-bladed with a scabbard of cowhide and a grip of Irish Oak, yet it had weight and Catherine knew it. At first she had refused the offering. She was indebted to Patrick enough without accepting gifts, let alone one as precious as this. But Patrick had insisted – 'I am not of sentimental aspect' – and Catherine had taken the knife. Now she treasured it as she did the words with which it belonged.

Catherine, Maude and Conall make their way along a narrow track. To one side is the Atlantic Ocean – contained by the bay and softly spoken today – to the other, hills with deep green slopes laid out like favourite velvet gowns. The rain stops and starts again. Progress is slow, but Catherine is happy. Eventually they reach a ruin.

'This is Kilgeever Abbey,' says Conall and Catherine is surprised to hear him speak.

The roof of the abbey is largely intact and the building looks as though it has only recently fallen into disrepair. Moss grows on the broken walls and it is a structure that appears to be a permanent feature of the landscape, as though it has emerged organically from the earth. As they stand at halt and stare at its remains, Catherine takes from her purse two plums. She gives one to Maude and they suck on them greedily, exchanging playful glances as they do.

They turn off the track and head to the shore through clumps of couch grass. At the sea, Conall dismounts and Catherine follows suit. Maude tries too and, toppling, is caught by her tutor. The clouds are higher now, the rain less threatening than drizzle. There are islands, of sorts, half-submerged in the bay; to the right and left, barely visible in the distance, rise hills and mountains. There is a narrow beach of stones, and from this a small wooden quay juts into the water. Tied to the quay is a rowing boat. The three of them secure their horses and Catherine and Maude climb into the boat. As Conall pushes them off, the rain stops again. Now a mist envelops the drumlins of the bay. Maude continues her chatter, the words skipping over the quiet surface of the water like swifts on a pond. 'Can I go to sea?' she asks and Catherine says 'I don't know. That's a difficult question. It's possible I suppose. Would you like to go to sea?'

'I would like to go to Spain. And maybe Portugal. I could too. And I am good at chess!'

'We shall have to see,' smiles Catherine.

They alight at Clare Island's small stone harbour. Catherine tells Conall they will continue by themselves and will be back within the hour. She neither knows nor cares if this is accurate. Conall looks frustrated, but Catherine hasn't posed any question and so he acquiesces. A light rain starts again. The island is rocky. There are mountains, their tops in cloud. Catherine and Maude take a path past a stone tower. It is squat and unlovely but standing as it does on raised ground, imposing too.

'This is another of Gráinne's castles,' says Catherine, partly to herself. They continue along a sheep track, parallel to the shore, keeping in sight of the bay to their left. Maude walks next to Catherine on wet grass and she struggles to hold her footing. Catherine instinctively reaches out to hold her hand then withdraws it: instead she manoeuvres Maude in front of her and they walk in single file. Patrick has told her the walk may be tiring and it is. Even though the day is largely still, a chill creeps into their marrow.

Eventually they reach St Brigid's. It is a simple church that sits on a cliff overlooking the bay; two white-habited nuns – are they Cistercians? – are tending gravestones in the graveyard. They squint

23

at Catherine and Maude as their bodies form from mist. 'Good morning,' says one, 'can I help you?'

'We are here to pay our respects.'

The nun nods. Catherine and Maude are shown into the abbey and Catherine's good mood is washed over and away by something more subdued. On the walls are dragons with thin wings, tails like whips and long claws, dragon slayers carrying lances. There is a coat of arms with a proud red boar. As she had been the previous evening, when she saw first the Atlantic, Catherine is awed. She is accustomed to religious spaces but there is something about the quiet in the abbey that is profound. It suggests safety, as though this place is a sanctuary, somewhere offering more than just a comfort for the Holy. Maude is affected too; at the tomb she catches her breath. Catherine bows her head and Maude follows suit. They stand in silence for a minute before Catherine says 'we should say a prayer' and they do. As they finish their devotion, Catherine's thoughts are interrupted by a scratching sound and a movement in the corner of her eye. It is a hare, its coat full and gleaming, that has somehow found its way into the chapel. The hare fixes Catherine with a bright and penetrating gaze and Catherine is transfixed. Maude too. Then the animal is gone.

They make their way back to the path, and retrace their steps to Gráinne's castle, through drizzle, without speaking. As they come into sight of the tower, Maude says 'That was sad. And not sad.'

'I know. It felt as though she was there with us and that we were all alone. And the hare. It was almost as if it was a sign.'

'When I was standing there, I thought about my mother.'

'I'm sorry.'

Maude does not respond. Catherine wonders if she has done the right thing in bringing her to the island. The trip has certainly been draining. Yet Maude isn't upset, at least not obviously so; her expression is unreadable. Catherine puts her arm round Maude's shoulders as they walk. Maude pulls away. 'There's no need,' she says.

Conall is wet and cold and hides his delight at seeing Catherine and Maude return. On the row back to the mainland, Maude hangs her arm over the side of the boat, trailing her hand in the water of the bay. When he notices, Conall stops rowing. He leans forward and shouts at the little girl: 'Sit still! I'll not have you going overboard!' There is anger in his voice and something else, something that might be fear. Maude looks at Catherine, but there is nothing Catherine can do. Not that she isn't concerned. The ill-temper of Conall's tone reminds her of Patrick that morning, when he had said that Maude was 'very important' to Theobald, and Catherine wonders if there is a reason for their proprietorial attitude towards Maude.

By the time she and Maude and Conall arrive back at the mainland and untether their impatient horses, the safety of the abbey seems far away and she is forced to consider more pressingly the reason for her presence – and that of Maude – at Rockfleet Castle.

Back at the castle in late-afternoon, the commotion has subsided but the atmosphere remains charged. A temporary stable has been erected and is full of horses. Theobald's men sit outside their tents, around a brazier. In a huddle around another are more armed men, standing with proud pikes and new muskets, the steel of their helmets and breastplates polished. This group has unfurled a standard, which they hold at an angle where it may be discerned in the encroaching gloom. It is a double-headed black eagle on a yellow background: while Catherine and Maude were at the island, John Browne of the Neale has arrived.

Inside the entrance hall, they are met by the smell of wet leather and cooking meat. They bump into Theobald who has clearly been awaiting their return, and Maude bows her head. Theobald is still dressed up but his plume is already less than proud.

'You have just crossed to the island?'

'Yes, Lord Mayo. To the abbey.'

'And may I ask why?'

'I had a mind to introduce Maude to your great grandmother.'

'Did you indeed.'

'You do not think this is to be recommended?'

'I do not.'

'– but –'

'– and that is the end of it. You have been brought here to do my bidding, nothing more.'

'I'm afraid I do not know yet what is required of me in that regard.'

'That is because you had no need to know. And now you do. Tomorrow you will meet with my guests. They will ask you about the girl and you will instruct them in her education, her disposition. You will tell them she is a fine and willing young lady of estimable character. That is what is required of you. *In that regard.*'

Theobald glares at Catherine. Slowly, the truth of the situation reveals itself; now she understands. So this is why she and Maude are at Rockfleet – Maude is to be promised in marriage. Of course! How had she not realised? So preoccupied had she been with one particular aspect of the girl's fortunes, she had neglected the activity in the wings. For a moment Catherine is furious with herself, then she realises this is no time for self-recrimination. She edges between Theobald and Maude, willing him to retire. He takes one step backwards, looks first at Catherine and then at his daughter. Up and down, up and down. Then he turns on his heel and walks away, in pitty-patty steps across the flagstoned floor.

26

That evening, Maude is waiting for Catherine. Catherine's chair sits next to hers, in front of the fire. 'I've got something for us to drink,' says Maude and she gestures to a jug of buttermilk on the floor. She produces two enormous wooden goblets embedded with cabochons.

'Where did you find those?'

'I took them from the kitchen. Don't worry. No-one will notice they are gone.'

'I do hope not,' says Catherine, but she knows her displeasure is unconvincing. Her mood is buoyant. She began the evening unsure how to process the news of Maude's forthcoming betrothal, but the anxiety she felt was washed away by nervous anticipation: tonight she will share the next instalment of Gráinne's story! She sits in the chair, leans over her elbows on her knees, her hands together as if in prayer. 'And now. Where were we?'

'The story of Gráinne is to be sipped and rolled about the tongue.'

'Ah yes! But of course it is! By now dear Maude, Gráinne is growing quickly older and more attuned to the expectations of her station. She has conquered the sea by her will and many men by her charms and is attending to the role of wife and woman of the clan. It is at this point that her tale takes on a different aspect. If the story of her childhood was one of her determination to overcome the barriers of men, so now she was impelled to prove herself a worthy victor of that struggle. First however, she was made to endure a passage of life more tragic than most could bear.

It began in Iarthar Chonnachta. In Iarthar Chonnachta there was strife. The English were to blame of course, for as I have come to see the English are most nearly always to blame, even on such occasion as the trouble has an Irish face – not least because their subjugation of Ireland and the Gaels is now centuries old. On this occasion the trouble was fomented by the English Queen. Her name was Elizabeth and she was born close in time to Gráinne and was almost her equal too, in the manner by which she imposed herself upon those who would deny her what she considered her due. That these two women shared such a force of will might explain how it was that each came to be defined – in part at least – by their relationship to the other.

If Elizabeth was happy to treat the fires in Connacht with oil, the trouble had its source with the actions of her father King Henry. Henry was the rapacious king of a rapacious kingdom, a man of the Devil who denied the word of God and built his power instead on conquest and theft and plunder. For many years before Gráinne's birth he had set about despoiling the traditions of the Gaels and the honest and loyal character of Irish men, in the name of an English Ireland. Has anyone told you of the 'amiable persuasion' of submit and regrant? No? Then listen well, for it will place the later actions of Grace O'Malley into a frame. It was thievery, no more no less, the seizure of Irish land and property at the point of a halberd, to be returned for proclamations of loyalty to the English Crown. Henry also introduced English laws and executed Gaels with impunity and then, to compound his wickedness, the conquest was prosecuted by more subtle means. In County Dublin there were fenced off towns and pasture on land known as The Pale, where English was taught and English sung and laws in written English made; further afield English-speaking English farmers were implanted on the most fertile Irish soil. The idea was to drive those Gaels who would not succumb to English rule to inhospitable lands beyond The Pale, "as dogs return to their vomit and as swine to their dirt and puddles." These plantations are how we come to be conversing now in the English tongue.'

From the floor below, there is guffawing. The meeting with the men of the Neale must be going well. Catherine glances in the direction of the stairs but Maude is not to be distracted.

'Would Gráinne have spoken English? Or Gaelic?'

'Each, at times, though it is likely her English was not good. It is said she had a facility for Latin and French though.'

'As do I!'

'Indeed! Not that such sophistication was of consequence to the English. Nor yet to certain of her kin. Although Elizabeth had at her call a number of bloody stewards whose authority was constrained only by their ambition, she could also draw on native antipathies. For centuries clans had been entangled in conflicts of bloodlines and steel and the English Queen knew just how to play these enmities to her advantage. One such affair unfolded in Iarthar Chonnachta, where the O'Flahertys were engaged in a benighted Irish hey with the Joyces of Maam, Cloghbrak, Tourmakeady and Cong. The two families had long mistrusted one another, with dispute over livestock following dispute over pasture, but despite the occasional intimidation, little had lately become of their discord. Until, that was, the intervention of Elizabeth's men.

At the centre of their plan to divide the O'Flahertys and the Joyces was Gráinne's husband Donal. For all that he was devoted to his wife and a man of oft-ignored tender-heartedness, Donal the Cock, Donal of the Battles was stronger in the arm than in the head. And so it was that shortly after the birth of Murchadh, an agent of the English was paid to ply his malicious trade in Ballynahinch and to pit him against the Joyces. His ruse was as simple as it was effective. Posing as a former Joyce foot soldier, he entered onto O'Flaherty land with stories of the theft of Donal's cattle. At the same time he made counsel with the Joyces and, claiming to have the ear of Donal himself, made mischief of a similar bent. With Donal and the Joyces thus inflamed, the fires of hatred were but a short distance away. Shortly after the impolitic Donal had made a public pronouncement of his desire to squash the rival family like a bug, he was ambushed by his rivals whilst out hunting, and butchered with several of his most trusted men.

This foul act cast Gráinne into despair, rent her heart asunder and dimmed the fiery wonder in her eyes. She was in that moment a broken woman. Her time with Donal had led her to the fancy that she might enjoy a life of contentment; now there was a realisation that she would be afflicted for the remainder of her three score years with a wretchedness that was not of her making. First however she had to bid her happiness a more formal goodbye. She returned to the hill Binn Ghuaire, whereupon she and Donal had consorted, and there, alongside the ancient stone that stands on its untroubled slopes, she buried her embroidery and Donal's lambskin glove. Then she withdrew to Bunowen Castle, to compose a caoineadh to mark the passing of her beloved. For seven days and seven nights she paced her quarters pouring her torment into an elegy that ebbed and flowed like creation itself.'

Maude's eyes widen. 'I would like to read this poem. May I? Please?'

'Alas, no copies of Gráinne's writing remain. It is not considered seemly for females to experiment with a quill, no matter their standing. Have I not told you that?'

Maude nods ruefully.

'You can imagine it though. And what it meant to her. Because this heartfelt cry aside, she was granted no time to grieve. The Joyces took Donal's death as a sign that their dispute with the O'Flahertys – the passions of which had been so callously heightened – may be settled in their favour. Approaching Donal's Castle of the Cock on Lough Corrib, they expected it to fall without resistance and to accede to the O'Flaherty land. But they had failed to reckon with Gráinne Ni Mháille. In her anguish, a cornered Gráinne found there stirred within her breast a new determination. If she did not prove the equal in combat of the Joyces, the memory of her husband would be as naught, her family's reputation sullied. And so she prepared, for the first time, for battle. And what a sight that was! Resolute and fearsome in cloak and robe and cuir bouilli, her scian by her side, she became less the charming Fionnabhair than her warlike mother Meadhbh, the ancient Queen of Connacht. For hours the Castle of the Cock was nearly overcome but Gráinne repulsed the Joyces again and again, with nothing but a handful of O'Malley and O'Flaherty men at arms and the spirit of a widowed queen. Finally she took lead from the roof of the castle and had it melted and poured down onto the heads of the assailants, whereupon they withdrew and were pursued and routed.'

Just then, a log on the fire hisses and spits an ember onto Catherine's dress. She brushes it off and the action moves her out of the depths of Gráinne's story. Instead she is suddenly aware of the effect of the words on her body: she is hot; she has edged her chair closer to Maude's, so close that their legs are nearly touching; her heart is beating quickly. Catherine takes a long breath. Pours some buttermilk for her and Maude, takes a swig. The drink is greasy and ever so slightly sour and Catherine is able to gather herself in the moment once more. When she continues, her delivery is more measured.

'After the vanquishing of the Joyces, the Castle of the Cock was renamed Hen's Castle and Gráinne returned to Clare Island. There, bereft and distraught she sought unlikely balm for her riven heart. A shipwrecked man named Hugh de Lacy, the son of a Wexford merchant, washed up on the shores of Achill Island and Gráinne took him for a companion in love. De Lacy was fully fifteen years her junior, but he was not cowed by her demeanour or reputation and the pair comported like ordinary lovers, in a manner that was blessed distraction for the grieving Gráinne. Yet there would be no lasting escape. Barely weeks into their union, De Lacy was butchered by the McMahons of Ballycroy, for the crime of his association with the now notorious O'Malley. Gráinne's mood was blackened still further by this most devilish of actions and she vowed to take amends in kind, to 'darken the skies of those who have darkened mine.' On the Feast of the Assumption, she heard tell a number of the McMahons would make a pilgrimage to the monastery on Caher Island. She sailed to meet them there and set about them with no quarter and continued to Doona Castle in Blacksod Bay whereupon she torched their fortress and put all in it to the sword. And so it was that Gráinne Ni Mhaile, Gráinne the Bald, became The Dark Lady of Doona too.

Her new reputation was a comfort of sorts. She was at least proving herself alongside violent men and in doing so finding her place in the world. But it was also a burden. She knew that the murders of those closest to her were a harbinger of worse to come. The lackeys of Elizabeth continued to pit Irish men against Irish men, clan against clan and O'Malley lands were rich in cattle and horses and the most fertile soil in Connacht. As such Gráinne was under threat from many sides, from those who coveted her influence to those who feared its spread. This ceaseless encroach of her enemies forced her to change tack. Her horizons narrowed from the boundless possibilities of all the corporeal realm to the lands over which she ruled, the seas through which she plowed. Like Elizabeth she was bound now not by her dreams but by her duty to her family. Where lately she would have responded to the threats with the snarl and goring of the cornered boar, now she sought a less bloody path. No more would she allow her hand to be forced, no more would she merely react to situations that were as elemental as the wind or rain – instead she would look further ahead, to the events of her past. As a young girl she had excelled at seeing the rocks beneath the sea and in manoeuvring around them with a steady nerve and it was this experience she would draw on in her quest to consolidate her power.

'Nothing but the actions of men have brought me low,' she declared, 'and though I must match them I must also reject their hold on my response.'

It was time to show she could fight Elizabeth and all others who would do her harm, with wit and prudence as well as the sword.'

Extract from The Two Queens, a play by 'Christopher Brady'

Greenwich Castle, London. A room furnished with a table and two chairs. A bottle of wine and two silver goblets are on the table. Queen Elizabeth, in royal robes, walks up and down

ELIZABETH:
[Sings]
Now is the month of maying,
When merry lads are playing, fa la,
Each with his bonny lass
Upon the greeny grass, fa la.

The door is knocked

Who is it?

BURGHLEY:
Lord Burghley. Your Majesty is well?

ELIZABETH:
I am looking forward to receiving my guest. You have news of her arrival?

BURGHLEY enters
[Earnestly]
I do, Your Majesty. The Irish pirate put anchor in the Thames an hour ago, as brazen as the day.

ELIZABETH:
The 'Irish pirate'?

BURGHLEY:
It is a name by which she has been known for some time.

ELIZABETH:
She goes by others too.

BURGHLEY:
[Hastily]
Is she not a pirate? She commands ships that steal and men that pillage.

ELIZABETH:
As do I.

BURGHLEY:
With all due respect Your Majesty, the circumstances are different.

ELIZABETH:
That is for me to judge, not you. And we have had this conversation. My guest is here to discuss a matter of state, an undertaking more commonly associated with Lords than pirates. I would suggest you show her a little courtesy.

BURGHLEY:
[Softly, or turning from her]
I'll bear it in mind.

ELIZABETH:
I wish you would. I am inclined to give her a fair hearing. Divine the contents of her heart and stomach, if you will.

BURGHLEY:
[Turns to look on the Queen, holding before him a knife]
Of course. Although before you do I would warn you that we searched her at the entrance to your quarters, and discovered this, hidden in the folds of her dress.

ELIZABETH:
[Snatches it from him]
I see.

BURGHLEY:
Should I have her taken to the tower?

ELIZABETH:
Maybe .
[Musing a little]
But no. There is sense, is there not, in taking a weapon into the den of one's enemy? So I think I will grant her this error of judgement.

BURGHLEY:
[Claps his hand to his breast]
Really? I would counsel caution.

ELIZABETH:
And I would disregard your counsel. What are the chances of this 'pirate' carrying two knives about her person?

BURGHLEY:
Your Majesty?

ELIZABETH:
Negligible, I would imagine.

BURGHLEY:

I scarcely think...

ELIZABETH:

I am aware of what you think, and you should know by now that I do not share your concerns. We have wasted enough time - please show my guest in. And see to it the fire is at its fullest.

BURGHLEY *tends to the fire*
Exit.

Wednesday, Rockfleet Castle

It is mid-morning and Catherine and Maude are summoned to the hall. Catherine is wearing a silk dress that Theobald has provided for her and it feels unusual against her skin. She is curious about what happens next but, unsure of her feelings on the matter, is unable to put her thoughts into words. As a consequence she has also been unable to provide any useful information to an inquisitive Maude, saying only of the meeting 'It won't last long.' This is reassuring but emptily so and she is aware that her other recent attempt at reassurance – about the trip to Rockfleet – was to some degree empty too, but what is she to do?

At the entrance to the hall stand two pikemen. In the hall there is a long oak table, beneath two coats of arms suspended from the ceiling. One is the familiar red cross and rampant lion of the Bourke's, the other the O'Malley boar. At the head of the table, in high-backed chairs, sit an agitated Theobald and his sullen son Miles. On one side of the table is John Browne of the Neale. Next to him is his son John Browne – a mere boy, five, maybe six years older than Maude – and next to him a man in a military sur coat whose name Catherine doesn't catch. Almost everyone except for Patrick and the soldier is draped in finery; there are plumes in felt hats, with collars and cuffs of lace, there are ribbons in hair. Only Theobald also looks bedraggled.

Catherine and Maude sit next to Patrick, who doesn't turn his head. John Browne and his son regard Catherine and Maude with a disinterested hauteur. The men around the table begin talking. They discuss Ireton's march on Limerick and the waning influence of Ulick Burke: 'a man whose time has gone,' says the younger John Browne and Theobald agrees; 'a champion of none but Ulick Burke' says the elder John Browne and Theobald agrees. These are observations of the sort that Catherine routinely shares with Patrick and she looks around the table. She notices that Miles Bourke contributes nothing. Why is he there? For decoration? It is odd, but not odd enough and soon she is bored. Maude too. She sits next to Catherine, still and unmoved. Catherine reaches for her hand and holds it in the little girl's lap. Maude stares straight ahead, sometimes raising her eyes to the standards and Catherine imagines her regarding the goldwork with a critical eye.

Eventually, the conversation takes a turn. English surveyors have been seen around Westport, says the elder John Browne, mapping out land and property. At last! Something of interest! Catherine lets Maude's hand go, leans a little forward.

'This is why we are here,' continues John Browne. 'The time is nearly on us when Charles' adventurers receive their recompense. It cannot be long before the confiscations start. Irish land for English gamblers –'

'– and Irish fellow travellers –

'– 'twas ever thus.'

'Indeed. And we will both lose, you and I. If only Kilkenny had shown more teeth – '

'– It is no use looking back. Besides. They too were in Charles' pocket. No, we are right to seek our own security. Which brings us to the matter in hand. A bond between the Brownes and Bourkes will be a good thing.'

'Some might say it is overdue.'

'Now now. Let's not fool ourselves that it is anything other than expediency that brings us here.'

Theobald feigns affront, may be affronted, perseveres. 'I understand yours is a wealthy and noble Clan but the Bourkes bring much to the table too. You will be aware that ours is a proud history.' At this, he nods towards the Ó Mháille standard.

'About that,' says the older John Browne. 'The girl's Ó Mháille blood. I would hope it does not betoken the manner of her actions.'

'As I have said,' says Theobald, 'we take pride in our ancestry. But I assure you my daughter's character is beyond reproach in that regard. On which subject I would like to introduce her tutor, Catherine Brady. Mistress Brady has been in the employ of my family for three years.'

Catherine clears her throat. Her mouth is dry. She feels as if she is on stage, with lines to deliver to an audience that has written the script. She is surprised to feel herself almost smiling. It is not with pleasure, more likely nerves. She wonders if this introduction – her presence? – is usual in situations like this. She hears herself saying what she has been told to say: 'Maude is studying Latin and French. Her needlework is exemplary. She is a polite girl and she desires to please her elders.'

The introduction is forced and the John Brownes are less than rapt. They nod and brush the sleeves of their suits, the legs of their breeches. Theobald leans forward, gawping, in expectation of a response which they decline to give.

'She has long legs,' says the father Browne in a stage whisper, 'so she may be inclined to be skittish.'

'How long, I wonder,' says the Browne son, 'before she can be put to the bull?'

They laugh. Catherine blanches. Sitting next to her, Maude – comprehending, uncomprehending, comprehending – seems to shrink. It is as though she has felt a thousand bereavements in a single moment. Under the table Catherine grasps her hand again. It is hot and sticky. Catherine might be angry, but then Theobald might say something, or Patrick, and they don't; it isn't their fault but what's the use? So she sits instead, like Maude, struck dumb. Theobald clears his throat.

'Very well. Mistress Brady, you may leave us. Maude, you will remain.'

Catherine returns her room and lies on her bed. She needs to clear her head. The meeting with the John Brownes has left her low and with many questions. Events are moving too quickly. No, it is not so much that. Events are always moving quickly in Mayo. Rather it is despite this, she has always imagined there to have been constancies too, whereas since her arrival at Rockfleet it seems there are none. Because now everything that matters to her – her position, the welfare of Maude – seems to be in motion.

Everything except Patrick. Catherine takes a deep breath, wills herself sanguine. Her friend has been difficult of late, but she knows why: she has found Rockfleet hectic and he must have too. Despite this, beneath his newly terse manner he is, she knows, unmoving. Amongst the motion, he remains a constant: this is the nature of the man. More practically, he has the ear of Theobald, is party to his motivations, his plans for Maude. No-one knows better the intricacies of the politics and history of Mayo. Yes, she may be on rutted ground but with Patrick's help she will find a way through it; through his friendship she will discover the answers to the questions she is posed.

That evening as the rain splats against the small window in the thick castle walls, Maude tells Catherine she does not want to marry John Browne. 'I don't like him. He has weasel eyes.'

Catherine weighs her words. 'You will grow to like him.'

'I won't.'

'You will.'

'I won't.'

'You may. And besides. Your father requires it. It is important to him.'

'But I don't want to.'

'I'm afraid you must.'

'But I don't want to.'

'I understand your reservations, but you must have faith that it will turn out for the best, really you must. You do not have to take my word for it, either. There is someone else who may be able to help. A good man who might give you cause to change your mind. I will ask him his opinion on the matter.'

'It does not matter what anyone says,' says Maude, 'I do not wish it.'

'Then what do you wish?'

'I do not know. But I know it isn't this.'

'It is hard Maude, I will grant you that. But you must not be hasty in your response. I propose you look again upon the situation in the morning, when your aspect will have brightened on account of the mere passage of time. And whilst we are waiting...'

'Are you going to tell me more of Gráinne?'

'I certainly had a mind to. Do you not wish that either?'

'I don't know. I think I may be unable to leave this world tonight.'

'That is for me to worry about,' says Catherine. 'Remind me of our place in the tale.'

Maude musters a thin smile. 'Gráinne is behaving like a man and wants to be more cunning.'

Catherine laughs. 'That is one way of putting it. Come. Let us continue.'

The two of them sit in their now usual spot before the fire. Catherine puts a finger to her lips and readies herself; even more so than before, Maude is in need of the succour that only Gráinne can provide.

'Tonight Maude, I want to tell you how Gráinne – who had tired of spilling blood in the pursuit of the respect of men – turned her hand to the fortunes of her family and to navigating more peaceably the fealties of Irish Clans and Englishmen, as if they were the drumlins of Clew Bay. It was not enough that she should prove herself as violent as men but their equal in politics too. In this she proved adept, but only after she had secured her renown for all time by a happenstance less contrived. Shortly after her return to Mayo, her father – the Black Oak Ó Máille – died. Gráinne did not mourn his passing for his death had been long expected and she had by this time few tears left to shed over the loss of someone close. Besides there were more pressing matters with which to engage.

In accordance with the Brehon Law, the Black Oak's successor as chieftain of the Ó Máille clan would be chosen by a gathering of the clan's derbfine. You may have heard of the derbfine, Maude – it comprises wise men with trusted judgement in such matters, whose word is not to be opposed. But Gráinne was not prepared to wait upon their deliberations. Instead she moved with purebred grace and speed and declared herself the new chieftain, the position she had coveted since she had been a little girl. Although she was both politically prepared and suited in spirit for such a move, the feat was audacious and undreamed of. Just imagine! A woman the chieftain of a clan! A weaker vessel more powerful than those who would thrust her to the wall! Why, this act alone would ensure her notoriety for the ages, for Gráinne was now the equal in status – a queen by any other name – as her great rival Elizabeth.

Yet your Gráinne was barely started on her newly chosen path. Her second act was to take another husband, less for love than matters of land and influence and power. It is for such reasons that you have been promised to John Browne, and although the arrangement of marriage is occasionally vexed, it has also sense to recommend it. The name of Gráinne's new husband was Richard Bourke and he was to be the Tánaiste of Mayo's MacWilliam Bourkes.'

Maude nods, slowly at first, then with increasing vigour.

'That's right. This is where your great great grandfather enters Gráinne's story. Richard was a wise choice for the newly peaceable Chief of the O'Malleys. He was besotted with her and had courted her affections for many years, pursuing her relentlessly with gifts and declarations of his desire. Despite his nickname – he was known as Risdeard an Iarrain – Richard in Iron – because of his habit of wearing a suit of chain mail – he was a pragmatic man, "a lover of quiet and civility". He was also a man of considerable wealth. For many years Bourke had practised the art of diplomacy, which had protected him from the excesses of the perfidious, and his lands had expanded until they encompassed the whole of the north of Clew Bay. Included in them was a property called Carrigahowley. Or, to call it by a name you may recognise, Rockfleet Castle.

The harbour here at Rockfleet is deep and ideally situated for one who wished, as Gráinne, to command the seas of the bay and beyond. Before long she had built up a fleet of galleys of Murrisk oak, each to carry seventy men with thirty at oar. She sailed these vessels out into the Atlantic, taxing local merchants and demanding fish and goods for passage, and she laid waste to seagoing traffic further south, in Galway Bay. Soon she acquired yet another name, The Sea

Queen of Connacht. Despite her best intentions however, and the influence of Richard in Iron, it was proving difficult to escape the grip of her warlike reputation.

On occasion this served her well. After giving birth to a son, Tiobóid a Búrc – Tibbot Bourke – whilst returning from a trading expedition to Spain, her galley was set upon by pirates from the Barbary states. Her men became shrivelled in the face of the long curled beards and pistols of their dark-skinned assailants and it was only Gráinne who prevented the taking of the ship, emerging from below decks with an arquebus and her babe in arms and rallying her crew to repulse the Barbary pirates. There were also, as ever, men from closer to home who were eager to tilt at the chieftain of the Clan O'Malley. One such was of a particularly treacherous nature. His name was William Óge Martyn fitz Thomas and he was the High Sheriff of County Galway. When Gráinne's sovereign mastery of Clew Bay caught the attention of the Irish Lords to the south, William Thomas marched on Rockfleet and sought to capture the O'Malley stronghold. Again, after suffering reverses, Gráinne stiffened the spines of her men and Thomas was repulsed, pursued and sent back to Galway with his weasel tail between his legs.'

'I knew it,' says Maude, quietly, as if to herself and Catherine presses on.

'Isn't she remarkable? And still, and still, there is more! Another incident involved the residence in Dublin Bay of the Baron Howth. After a trip to the seat of English power in that fair yet tangled city, Gráinne approached the castle and requested supplies for her return to Mayo. For reasons unbeknownst to all but him, the Baron declined to furnish Gráinne with food or water; worse, he barred the gates of his castle and closed his tath-blocked ears to her entreaty.

Gráinne took pains to mull her choices and dwelt until dawn upon the most conciliatory of actions, but her sense of injustice had been revived. Chancing upon the Baron's heir on land between the castle and the sea, she took him prisoner and suggested to the Baron that he reconsider his response. The Baron, suitably chastened and alarmed, declared that from that moment on there would always be an extra table laid at Howth for visitors who strayed onto his land and asked of him good manners.'

At this point, Catherine pauses. 'Now listen, Maude. Before I go on, I should say that although Gráinne's life was one of many feats and perils, some of these tales may be wanting in their veracity. It is true, for instance, that there are several versions of this tale of Howth. But you will gather, I hope, by now, that this spoken history is all we have; no written account of your great great grandmother and her deeds have survived this passage of time, even though it is the merest. This is why it is so is difficult for us to judge to any useful degree; perhaps it is because most stories are told by men, of men, for men.'

Again, Maude nods. 'I have noticed this. At night, when my father is entertaining lords, there is sometimes a bard. But rarely one who tells of girls.'

'Indeed. Not that Gráinne paid heed to such polarity –'

'– polarity?'

'–we have not spoken of polarity? I must see to that.'

'Oh. Must we?'

'Haha! Don't worry, Maude – I meant when I have seen to the story. So. Where are we? Ah yes.

After twelve months of marriage, Gráinne once again demonstrated her acumen in honest manipulation. Although she remained loyal to Richard of Iron and he to she, she was not taken with him as a lover and took it upon herself to release him from their matrimonial contract. She summoned him to Rockfleet and there, denying him entry to the castle, called out from a first floor window – maybe that very one – "I dismiss thee!" This, according to the Brehon Law that she had prior cause to bend to her will, was all that was needed to dissolve their union.

Next she took advantage of her prowess at sea, which was such that even the English navy was belittled. In Munster, Irishmen were rebelling against Elizabeth in the name of their church. The native nobles required their kern and buanadha be stiffened by Scottish fighting men, and Gráinne ferried Hebridean redshanks and Gallowglass from Argyll to the shores of Tralee Bay. Such actions would have seen her hung and quartered but she was too wise to let her involvement in the enterprise be common knowledge. Moreover, she also played the English at their double-dealing game. The Lord Governor of Ireland at this time was a man by the name of Henry Sidney, and Gráinne simultaneously placed men and ships under his instruction. This was an offer that met, at first, with the required equanimity. "There came to me a most famous feminine sea captain called Grace O'Malley," declared the outwitted lickspittle, "and offered her service unto me, wheresoever I would command her, with three gallies and two hundred fighting men." Later, with the clans of Munster and Connacht remaining unruly, Sidney's desire to crush them led him to further grace Gráinne with his favour in return for the services that only she could provide. On one occasion he sailed with her to inspect the ocean-facing defences of Galway, a trip for which she was handsomely recompensed in gold.

The point here, Maude, is that it is possible to turn the most unpromising of situations to your advantage, have you only the wit and dexterity to see how this might be accomplished.'

'Have I the wit?'

'Most certainly. You might say it is a family trait, give or take the odd exception.'

'And the dexterity?'

'Of course! You have played cup and ball?'

'I have.'

'Then you can handle self-important men!

Alas, despite her skill in this regard, Gráinne's star was rarely blessed with fortune. Was it Sidney's gold that turned her head? It is possible. Whatever it was, she was soon to overplay her hand. Shortly after the reconnoitre of Galway, Sidney was replaced by another of Elizabeth's ennobled henchmen, Lord Grey de Wilton, a man of a considerably less biddable aspect. The timing was significant. The MacWilliam Bourke's relationship with their neighbours had of late descended into rancour and Gráinne had taken to plundering the latter's land and property. On this occasion her bold desire did not serve her well and after many successful forays she was taken captive by the Earl of Desmond's men and thrown into Limerick gaol. Desmond was no fool and recognising in his prisoner a prize beyond material value, arranged for Gráinne's transfer to Dublin castle in return for the support of a sympathetic de Wilton.

Once again – imprisoned, alone – Gráinne found herself in a position that would have broken lesser men. By now however she was more willow than oak. Pacing the floor of her cold stone cell, she bent and bent again, inured by infinite resource to privations that would have snapped lesser men in two. And so it was that just as prior adversity had made her formidable, so this made her more formidable still. On her release a year hence, she returned to Rockfleet, reinvigorated, and continued in her struggle to make fast her family's fortunes.

During her time in prison, the ailing Richard's authority as Tánaiste of the MacWilliam Bourkes had come under increasingly unscrupulous scrutiny. His power – good-hearted and benign – was under threat. With Gráinne free once more and the English distracted by the Holy War in Munster, she oversaw the display of two thousand Bourke and Ó Máille men at arms, cowing all who would take advantage of her tolerant husband. The show of strength bolstered Richard's claim and he was both recognised as the Chief of the MacWilliam Bourkes and ennobled by the English. Gráinne, then, was not only bold but selfless too in the actions she took to secure a future for her family. She saw that loyalty and sacrifice were not signs of weakness but another of the strengths she must show. Do you understand?'

'I think so.'

'Good. Because, Gráinne was strong.

By now her authority, underpinned by her blade-like sharpness in matters of tact, was unsurpassed in all of Connacht; she had become as unreachable for men who would do her harm as the sun and moon. For the first time since Donal's death she was happy too, or as happy as she could expect to be whilst still bearing that most terrible of losses. Her lands were fertile, her seas were bountiful and her family was safe and provided for. Eoghan had grown into a much-loved and loving son who was known for his wise counsel, Méadhbh was her mother's daughter, boisterous and brave, and although Murchdach had his father's impetuosity, he was sharp-witted and resourceful too. And, of course, there was Tibbot, a pragmatic young man in love like his mother with tide and wave.

Even the death of your great great grandfather, who slipped through infirmity to a natural end, could not bring this reborn Gráinne low. Indeed she read into his passing another opportunity. Citing laws that were neither wholly Irish nor wholly English but closer in fact to O'Malley fancy, she took for herself land and property that had once been his. It seemed then as though Gráinne had ascended to a place from which she could look down on the doings of less capable men, the bog of English Irish and Irish Irish enmity from whence she had emerged. But there were forces gathering over which even she could exercise no control.'

Extract from The Two Queens (continued)

Elizabeth sits, drinking from a goblet of wine.
Enter BURGHLEY, leading in Grace, richly attired

ELIZABETH:
[Stands]
Ah! Grace O'Malley, I do believe.
[Looking fixedly on her]
Or would you rather Grainne Ní Mháille?

GRACE:
Whichever Your Majesty pleases.

ELIZABETH:
Very good. Grace O'Malley then. I am pleased to meet you.

GRACE:
Likewise, Your Majesty, I'm sure.

BURGHLEY:
[After a pause, amazed]
You do not see fit to bend your knees before the Queen of England?

GRACE:
[Looking on Elizabeth, boldly]
I mean nothing by it. I am not in the habit of bending my knees before anyone.

ELIZABETH:
[Aside, softly]
A woman of independent spirit, I see.

BURGHLEY:
Ma-am? This cannot be a measure …

ELIZABETH:
[Turning from him]
I trust your journey was a pleasant one? The weather has been most inclement of late.

GRACE:
I am from the West coast of Ireland. It is no more nor less than I am used to.

ELIZABETH:
How very indomitable!

GRACE:
Merely honest, Your Majesty.

ELIZABETH:
Refreshing too. A little honesty will make for a more fulfilling joust than those I am accustomed to with Burghley here.

GRACE:
With respect, I am not here to joust.

ELIZABETH:
Not even with an uncorked lance?

GRACE:
I would rather we attend to business.

ELIZABETH:
[Plucks from her robes a handkerchief]
Very well. But before we start, I would like to give you this small gift. To demonstrate the spirit in which I would have us hold our discussion.

GRACE:
[Takes it up, looks on it, smiles]
Thank you.

BURGHLEY:
It is a handkerchief. I trust you are familiar with such an item?

GRACE:
I am. It is just that it is a most unusual gift. Though perhaps... ah, yes, timely.

GRACE *snots her nose on the handkerchief and casts it on the fire*

BURGHLEY:
[Angrily]
You would burn a gift from the Queen of England? I warned Your Majesty! More flagrant disrespect!

GRACE:
I'm afraid you are mistaken, My Lord. It is merely the custom in Connaught.

BURGHLEY:
A lie!

ELIZABETH:
[Looking on Grace]
It is?

GRACE:
I assure Your Majesty. We would not consider keeping such an item about our person.

ELIZABETH:
[Smiling]
Very well. Come. Sit down.

ELIZABETH:
[Sits down, beckons Grace to a chair]
Perhaps a custom of my own will do you good. Can I interest you in a little wine? To celebrate your journey here?

GRACE:
[Sits]
There is no need. As I said, the passage was bearable and took only a day.

ELIZABETH:
Surely it is closer to twenty years since we first locked horns?

GRACE:
You are right, of course. Alas, I must decline your offer. I would like to retain a clear head for our negotiations.

ELIZABETH:
[Turns her face away, then angrily]
I see. But there is something you should know. I am trying to show you what I consider to be your due regard, but my patience will be stretched only so far. I would remind you where you are. And point out that those who forget do not repeat their error of judgement.

GRACE:
[Looking fixedly on Elizabeth]
Perhaps I will take some wine after all.

ELIZABETH:
A wise decision. Burghley? If you please. Now. Shall we attend to the formalities? In which language would you care to conduct business? We can carry on in English or I can converse in the Popish tongue, but I have to confess that I know no Irish.

GRACE:
I am happy to continue in English. It is the language of power, is it not?

ELIZABETH:
Another honest observation.

GRACE:
Thank you, Ma'am-

ELIZABETH:
And one befitting a statesman too.
[Looking on Burghley]
Lord Burghley? You heard the 'Irish pirate'?

BURGHLEY:
[Sighs]
Ma'am.

ELIZABETH:
And so. A pirate, a statesman and unless I am mistaken, a potential ally. Am I right in saying that although you have long been an enemy of the English crown, you have come here today seeking an alliance?

GRACE:
[Musing a little]
That is certainly one way of looking at it. Although I would perhaps not recognise myself in your description.
Whilst it is true that I have been kidnapped by Englishmen and threatened with execution, my family subjected to continuous harassment-

ELIZABETH:
-all by the grace of God-

GRACE:

-I would consider myself less an enemy of your realm than a defender of my own.

ELIZABETH:

[Looking on Grace]
Really? A defender of your own? Have you not also been in dispute with the Kingdom of Ireland?

GRACE:

True again, Your Majesty. But only in the name of the Irish people, whose fealty is more to clan than crown.

ELIZABETH:

I see. But still. You need to convince me.

GRACE:

Of what, Your Majesty?

ELIZABETH:

That we have - despite your disregard for innocent handkerchiefs - more in common than divides us.

BURGHLEY:

If I may...

ELIZABETH:
[Hastily]
I have detained you long enough, Lord Burghley.
You may leave us.

BURGHLEY:
[Amazed]
Ma'am?

ELIZABETH:
[Turns away from Burghley, looks on Grace]
Lord Burghley?

Exit Burghley

Thursday, Rockfleet Castle

Catherine is enduring a wakeful night. The evening's storytelling was exhilarating in its way, but there were also complications and since the sun set she has been enveloped by doubt. She is unconvinced by the moving parts of Rockfleet. Her surroundings do not help. While it had initially provided her with a source of interest, her room in the castle has taken on an oppressive aspect. It is a small room with a small window and Gráinne is there and then gone, and sometimes mocks Catherine for her vacillations. And Catherine is vacillating. There is much in her head. She is in conflict with herself about Maude and Theobald and Gráinne and Patrick; the implications of the questions she has planned to put to her old friend are flickering like the shadows from candles against the wall.

Now she has had time to dwell, she finds herself vexed by Maude's planned betrothal, recalls an incident from long ago. It took place in Dublin and involved a friend of her father's, a printer. Her father had requested that as the man was a first time visitor, perhaps Catherine would like to introduce him to the city. Catherine was puzzled but agreed and she and the man were left unchaperoned for an afternoon. They visited St Patrick's Cathedral, sitting in a state of intriguing disrepair, and other places that Catherine has long forgotten. The printer was friendly enough and the time had passed convivially, until Catherine defended a dubious character of their mutual acquaintance with the observation that "God hath given him, one face, and he has made himself another". The line was one of her favourites but Catherine had not meant anything by it: the printer was not someone she had a desire to impress. As such she was surprised at the speed with which he made his excuses. It was only later that she discovered the situation had been contrived for the purpose of finding her a suitor and that her father wished her to be given in marriage. The outcome didn't please her father but then the exercise wasn't to her liking either. Even at that age, she had been wary of women who were conspicuously desirous of such male attention. It seemed as though this was merely a substitute for something more substantial.

Her experience of such arrangements then, was far from benign. Not only that, but although the agreement with the Brownes is, in practice, little more than a declaration of intent, Maude is still a child and this does not sit well with Catherine. Because as their relationship has developed, so Catherine realises just how she is relishing its growth. Maude remains her responsibility of course – a pupil, a mourning, vulnerable little girl – but there is something about the ease with which they are now conversing that means that Catherine has begun to cast her in the role of companion too.

Maude is innocent and perceptive, guileless and full of guile and Catherine hasn't enjoyed such a bond since her own childhood. True, she is close to Patrick, but their relationship remains coloured, as it has been from the outset, by the taint of an entanglement of an entirely different nature. He has never directly suggested as much of course, but there have been occasions – she remembers a trip to Brackloon, an afternoon of riding instruction – when she has felt the air move by a quietly whipped tongue and realised others have. How are she and Patrick viewed by others? What is the truth of their friendship? Whereas with Maude, of course, the relationship is altogether simpler.

Which begs a question. After the initial shock had passed, Catherine had seen fit to encourage Maude to accept the arrangement being made for her. Why was this? She would like to consider it a response that was out of character, but if this was so, then where had it come from? Was it a failure of courage? A meek acceptance of the futility of opposing what was destined to be? A recognition that any dissent would have no effect, could be nothing more than a gesture? Or was it something different again? Could it be that she has become inured to the idiosyncrasies of life beyond The Pale, has grown so used to the unsophisticated practises of Mayo, that she no longer views them as such without reflection? This would certainly explain her reaction to the hare that interrupted her reverie at Gráinne's tomb. She knows that Mayo was a land of superstition, and that such ancient stories were used to dampen the spirit of enquiry that she so cherished, and yet she has been unable to shake herself free of the idea that the creature was sent by someone, to test her fealty to the truths of her adopted land.

As she has when previously visited by doubt, Catherine returns to the woman that brought her to Rockfleet. She retrieves a bundle of silk beneath her bed, removes Gráinne's knife from its plain leather sheath. The blade is long and deadly. She closes her eyes and, seeking comfort or reassurance, places the knife in the context of the castle, in the corner of Gráinne's chamber, hanging from her belt on a hunt. It does not help. Rather it sets her yet more interrogations: did the weapon have significance or was it merely an everyday instrument? Had it been used to kill? From the stories Patrick told, the answer to the latter was obvious. A century ago, Mayo was a land of killers, and Gráinne had killed too. But then what was the relationship of the narrative of the Pirate Queen to the blood and flesh of Mayo?

Catherine is no longer sure. For all that they were told with passion and sincerity, Patrick's stories of Gráinne tied old Mayo in a series of neat bows, to be undone when he saw fit. Now Catherine is presenting her own packages to Maude. She has always intended the story to be instructive: Gráinne encounters obstacles, Gráinne overcomes; Maude is comforted, and, despite it all, and with her eyes wide open, accepts her lot. But what if Gráinne's life deserves more than such pat conclusions? What if she is trying to do too little with it? What if there is more to the tale than this? Or worse, less? What if the past was not instructive but something else entirely? Something so estranged from today that it could not teach us anything?

If only Theobald felt the same. Instead, he seems alarmed by Catherine's interest in the stories of his forbears. She has always known he was wary of her unorthodox teaching – he has, on occasion, remarked on this – but since she has introduced Maude to Gráinne Ni Mháille, the situation has worsened. Now Theobald talks to her as if she is a stranger or an enemy. This is disconcerting. It is also unnecessary. It angers her. She does not understand why Theobald should think like this about his great grandmother's life. His decision to decamp to Rockfleet was made with the intention of summoning Gráinne's legacy, using it to remind John Browne of the stature of the Bourke family, to give him an advantage in the negotiations surrounding Maude's betrothal; the O'Malley coat of arms is on prominent display in the hall where the discussions are taking place. Why then, should Catherine not also draw upon the story of Gráinne to try to give succour to the youngest Bourke? How and why is Gráinne's story good for one and not the other? And what, exactly, is the threat it poses to Theobald?

As Catherine's indignation flickers, she imagines he is frightened by Gráinne. Afraid of how the shadow of her life blots out the light of his own. Or perhaps he is scared of the past itself, the way it consumes the present, mocks its transience, belittles it with the vastness of death. This would explain his frantic motion; it is a desperate attempt to put distance between him and what has gone, to avoid being washed away by its relentless presence.

Whatever the reason for his disquiet, it has weakened Catherine's desire to stay in Castleburke. She has always assumed she would remain in Mayo until Maude was no longer in need of her tutelage. Now she questions that intention. After all, she has done what she set out to do in Mayo. Proved herself, risen to the challenge. Might she be better off returning to Dublin? Will that city's dissatisfactions mean less now she has tasted others? If the decision is not to be taken out of her hands, that is. Theobald may yet dispense with her services. She might yet be forced to return, before Maude is of an age.

The room grows lighter. Catherine rises, paces. Has she time to sleep before dawn? She needs to. More than that she needs Patrick. She flits again – where to now? – to her thoughts of earlier in the night and to the recollections of an ancient fancy. Back to her arrival in Mayo, the origin of their friendship. Had it been merely the stories that had got her through those days of merciless isolation? Or was it Patrick himself? She is unsure but either way, despite herself, she needs him. To dash her worries against his stoicism, her vacillations against his core.

At daybreak Catherine asks Patrick if he can join her for breakfast. He is to hold further discussions with Theobald and the John Brownes and demurs. Catherine spends the morning with Maude. They talk about Copernicus and St Paul, take on a little French. Maude seems distant once more. She does not concentrate. Catherine does not chide her. There is no mention of Theobald or Gráinne and Catherine is relieved. She is overtired. Her eyes hurt. The night before was a feverish, sobering experience and she needs space to breathe before she talks to Patrick.

The respite is short-lived. It is the afternoon. Theobald is hunting with the John Brownes, Maude is attending to her embroidery and Catherine and Patrick have taken the opportunity to walk along the sandy track to Westport before the rain comes. What is more, the suggestion had been his. 'I have some things to tell you,' he'd said, and she had divined from his tone that whatever it was pertained to the questions she had for him. She was buoyed by this, yet the exchange is not playing out as she would have liked. They have been walking for ten minutes and nothing of consequence has passed between them. Patrick has been as taciturn as he has since their arrival at Rockfleet. Catherine resorts to teasing.

'It's foxglove.'

'We say lus mor.'

'My preference is for foxglove.'

'That may be so. But it's lus mor.'

'Perhaps it can be both? Foxglove for me and lus mor –'

'–*Lus mor*'

'–*Lus mor* for you.'

'And there we have it. Once again. I am not in the mood for this.'

Catherine looks for signs of levity in Patrick's voice, finds none. She sighs. She is perplexed and frustrated. She glances at her walking companion, who stares straight ahead. How long will his ill-temper persist? 'Patrick? I'm sorry, but there are other matters to which I could be attending. This walk was your suggestion. I agreed because there are things we could usefully discuss. Equally, I am happy to do so on an occasion when your reluctance is less marked.'

Patrick continues staring. 'I am considering my words,' he says. 'We were…we have been friends for a long time, but the matter I wish to speak to you about is grave. You are forcing me to make choices I do not have.' He takes a long breath. 'Theobald and I have noticed your lack of enthusiasm for our negotiations with John Browne of the Neale. And I should warn you that Theobald is not to be trifled with in this regard. As I have told you before, the future of his land and property is threatened.'

'Theobald is all bluster, you must know that. I'm sure I can handle Theobald, under pressure or not.'

'This is different. There is much you do not know. He has moments when he is not himself. He has the terrors. Rages.'

'Really?'

'Something happened to him. Years ago, in the Confederate Wars. There was a massacre, near Shrule: a group of settlers, a bishop, on their way out of Mayo. The Second Viscount was there and Theobald too. No-one is sure of their involvement but Theobald was badly affected.'

'But that must have been ten years ago. When I met him in Dublin, he was a composed enough man. And well-regarded too.'

'That's as maybe. But it is important that you understand that circumstances have changed. These are confounded, bloody times. Life is cold-hearted and violent and short.'

'I do understand,' says Catherine, 'of course I do. I have heard of these arrangements before, in Dublin. It is just… She is very young.'

'In Dublin? I see. But this isn't Dublin. This is Mayo.'

'So Maude is too young in Dublin? But not in Mayo?'

'This is not a question you should ask. Accordingly, I will not answer it.'

'Very well. Answer me this then. What happens next?'

'I haven't time to discuss that now.'

'Then when? Tell me that, Patrick. Whatever is taking place, Maude is my charge.'

Patrick raises his eyebrows. 'Maude is your pupil. Again, there is a difference.'

'I have a responsibility for her welfare.'

'You do not.'

'I am paid to guide her as she comes of age.'

'You are paid to guide her in a set direction.'

Catherine compresses her lips, turns to look at the hillside. They pass a sucking bog, gorse. There is a faery tree. She has made no headway on the question of Maude's betrothal and needs to move the conversation on. But time is running out. As they continue along the path, the faraway tops of Nephin Beg are shrouded and the air turns colder; the rain is closing in. A murder of crows lands a short distance away. Patrick bends down, picks up a stone, throws it. 'Get away!' he shouts and the birds take flight.

First a hare and now a crow; foreboding. Catherine resists such thoughts, and tries again. Indulges Patrick, touches his arm. 'My! I had no idea you held such strong feelings for crows!'

'I don't like them. When Maewyn Succat fasted, the devil put the souls of demons into crows. They're an omen. They tell of the strength of the bad old ways, that we are never free of them.'

'Oh yes! I have heard that story! You told it to me, when I first arrived in Castleburke. Do you remember?' Catherine turns to look at Patrick. He tips his head back, closes his eyes and for an instant, there is something more than words between them, she is sure. It is the trust that can only come from shared experiences, a vindication of her faith in him.

'Of course,' he says. 'They were the stories that my mórai told to me.'

This is the Patrick whose friendship Catherine values so much. Attentive, softened. Almost wistful. She senses an opportunity. 'I think of them often. And of those times too. In my cottage, warm. The wine. The poetry – Tuileagna Ó Maoil Chonaire – do you remember? It meant a lot. They mean a lot.'

'Indeed.'

'Do you miss those times, I wonder?'

Patrick looks at the ground. Does not reply.

'It is no matter,' says Catherine. 'And yet sometimes I ask myself…'

'Ask yourself what?'

Catherine pauses – what to say next? – decides to be direct. 'About the stories. I mean if they mean so much, why are they not to be shared more widely? How is it that Theobald sees fit to draw on Gráinne's reputation, but has decided that Maude should not be afforded the same succour?'

Patrick frowns. The spell is broken. The opportunity, such as it was, has passed. 'What has Gráinne's story to do with Maude?'

'Come now. You know very well. Maude is a wonder but she is without direction. I thought she would benefit from hearing of such an ancestor, that it might help to ground her.'

'You thought a wilful child would be grounded by tales of Gráinne Mhaol?'

'Hmm. I see what you mean. But I will also confess I am surprised that Grace's story is not better known. I think it deserves to be told. It is a story of some importance, is it not. And yet in Dublin –'

'– in Dublin!'

'– in Dublin, no-one has heard her name. Do you not find that strange?'

'I do not. Gráinne's story is good for cowing blackguards who would take liberties with her bloodline and for stirring the passions of poets and low-born men. And for those of a sentimental mind who need the comfort of a fireside tale, of course. But that is as far as it goes. Her life was an exception, a one-off. A diversion. Her tale is an idle entertainment, signifying nothing. It has no relevance to the work of those who reside in Dublin and it is not suitable for the likes of Maude.'

'I am not sure I agree.'

'It is not for you to agree or disagree.'

'But does her story not *belong* to Maude?'

'It does not. It belongs to Theobald. As Gráinne belongs to Theobald. She is what he decrees. Her story is his to do with as he sees fit.'

'Is she not beyond the reach of Theobald? Part of this place? Part of this land, its grass, its earth? Does she not fall in its damnable rain?'

At this Patrick turns to glare at her, his face red with anger. 'Do not dare presume to tell me of this land! All of it, for as far as you can see, as far as you can imagine, is ours. And it will always be. Do you understand? Not yours. Ours. It is held together with our laws, our customs, it is made rich with our blood. This is why Maude will marry John Browne of the Neale. This is why you have no place peddling our stories. This is why you think you understand but you are wrong. Do you hear me? You do not understand. You will never understand. *Go hifreann leat!'*

Patrick waves his arms, dismisses Catherine, lopes back towards the castle. Catherine is distraught. She cannot gather her thoughts, turns her face up to the sky, as if the rain will somehow dampen the commotion in her head. It doesn't. She can scarce believe what has just happened. There is much to comprehend, too much to comprehend. Such violence, such bitterness; where has it come from? She walks slowly back towards the castle, past the cottages, the tents and braziers. The scene is suddenly foreign to her. Rockfleet is isolated in the mist, its stone as cold as the earth.

Her day does not improve. Later, in her room, she understands. Patrick said she is wrong and she is. What a fool she has been! She has been wrong all along. Wrong about him, wrong about their friendship, wrong about what he might provide. If Patrick had ever been there for her, if his presence alongside her had not been an illusion, he left her when they arrived at Rockfleet, never to return.

She is wrong about something else too. *All* this, he'd said, all this is ours, as it will always be. Catherine did not know what he meant by ours – does she not worship the same God? Speak the same tongue? – but she understands now, or at least imagines she might.

If she is right then there are constants besides Patrick, there are constants everywhere – Theobald is one, the custom and laws of Connacht another – and they provide Catherine with neither comfort nor security. There is no longer anything for her here.

Catherine is shaken to her essence by this realisation, engulfed by the shadows of its portent, seized by an absence, held tight by something that isn't there, by the impossibility of redemption, by the impossibility of release from this state that is now deathless. She is alone and this is the end of her adventure.

Catherine is late for that afternoon's Latin. Maude is sitting on her bed, staring out of the window at the rain. She turns hesitatingly to greet her tutor and Catherine gasps. There is a cut on the girl's forehead. Her cheek is swollen and discoloured, a livid purple, an affecting yellow. Her eyes are reddened through tears.

'My dear Maude! What happened to your face?'

'A man slapped me. Like this. Several times. He was wearing a big ring.'

'Who? I mean who would dare? Have you told your father?'

'He was one of John Browne's men, so my father did nothing.'

'Why did he strike you?'

'He told me he had heard I was to marry John Browne's son and I said I didn't want to.'

Catherine is shocked. Not by the violence – she knows the old saying that a man's mouth often broke his nose – but by the frightened confusion on Maude's bruised face. This is not right. She leaves the room, returns five minutes later. 'Here. I have something for you.'

She presents a bundle of silk to Maude. Maude is puzzled.

'It belonged to Gráinne,' says Catherine, as Maude unwraps the gift. 'I thought you should have it.'

'But why?'

'Because I fear you might have use for it one day.'

Maude stares at Gráinne's knife as if it were made of gold. And as she does so Catherine sees that her relationship with the girl has taken on a yet another aspect. Now they are bound together. By their circumstance here at Rockfleet, of course, by their friendship, but by more also. By their sex. By the story of Gráinne, even as its lessons – if that is what they are – flicker before them. In that moment, in Catherine's anger and despair, the story itself becomes something different too. Catherine had always intended to use Gráinne to show Maude that she could belong. Now she sees that Maude cannot belong because there is nothing for her to belong to; as Catherine is scrabbling on a limb, so the place Maude has in the way of things is not one fit for her. So Catherine will use what is left of Gráinne's story for a different purpose: to more obviously inspire the little girl. To embolden, not reassure, to show her there can be another way – there has to be another way – that there is always the promise of something new, the chance to live a little differently, whatever it might be. She owes the girl that much. And besides. Maude's room is small, its walls are thick, the window lets in little light; what else is there to be done?

A small fire barely smoulders but the room is hot. There is no sound from the rest of the castle. Maude is sombre, even as she clasps Gráinne's knife. Catherine knows that Maude is lost again and her spirit needs once more to be revived. She too is in need of an invigoration. Yet tonight there is no buttermilk and none of the animation that Maude has brought to earlier parts of Gráinne's story; tonight she has to try something else.

As Maude sits on the bed, Catherine challenges herself to put on a performance, as if on the stage at Werbergh Street, as if such a display might restore their optimism. She paces, considers the temper of her words. 'Maude, it is difficult, I know, but you must stay strong. There is little I can do of a practical nature but I will give my last breath to billow your spirit. Here, now let me tell you more of Gráinne, for you will have realised that hers is a story of no little inspiration. We have reached the point where her star was at its zenith.

Unfortunately all that meant to some was that it could plunge further than they had hitherto imagined possible. There was one man in particular among the butchers of dreams, the would-be enslavers of her soul, who sought her descent. His name was Richard Bingham, he was a fallen angel of that other Eden, and he was tasked by Elizabeth with bringing Connacht to heel.

When Bingham arrived in Connacht, his authority was unconstrained and he set about seizing a reputation designed to unnerve the most disputatious of Irish opposition. He arranged a council for all the clans in Mayo and when some of your family withheld their presence he destroyed their castle at Lough Mask; in County Clare he put the garrison of Castle Cloonoan to the sword, while in Galway the assizes saw fully seventy men sent to the gallows. But it was Gráinne against whom he wished to set himself.

For Bingham, Elizabeth bettered men by divine right whereas Gráinne ruled in defiance of all that was good and Holy. She was Irish too, a race he considered "never tamed with words but swords." And then there was the matter of her sex. The manner in which she dissented from the choreography of the dance was the root of much hostility. You have just seen this attitude made manifest at first hand, Maude, and it is a stubborn blight upon the character of our world. Gráinne was a warrior and Gráinne had, so Bingham thought, "imprudently passed the part of womanhood". Not only that but unlike the English queen, whose eye he hoped to catch, she was not abashedly female but a lover of nights carousing and swimming in rivers and reading poetry with men. Gráinne then was an outlandish woman who did not belong in Bingham's world; as such he would accept neither the actions of her family nor the borders of her realm.

It was not long before the two collided, with Bingham luring Gráinne into a bog of provocation, to draw from her an intemperate response. First he kidnapped Tibbot na Long, holding him in Ballymote Castle for a year. Then, following the death of Richard in Iron, he hanged the new Tánaiste, Edmund Bourke of Castlebar, to set that clan's latent rivalries in motion. Finally Bingham sprang his most heinous trap. He sent his brother John onto O'Malley land, supposedly for the purpose of a reconnoitre, where he approached Gráinne's son, the gentle Eoghan, and asked of him his hospitality. Eoghan was a good host and escorted the English to the island of Inishturk, Clew Bay, where he provided them with food and drink. Once there, cleaved from the security of his clan, hemmed-in by the sea and with scarce enough men to defend himself, he was overwhelmed by the treacherous interlopers, taken captive and murdered. The English claimed that Owen "being prisoner, made his escape and in pursuit was slain" but the lie did nothing to assuage Gráinne's grief.'

At this, a look of such dejection crosses Maude's face that Catherine stops her narration. 'No, no! It will be alright, God willed a hopeful resolution to Gráinne's travails! If there weren't I would not continue. It is just… it was taxing, Maude, as taxing then as it is now. But is it not the case that the dark is at its deepest before the dawn?'

Ha! Now she is resorting to cliché to cushion the truth, as if the truth were too much to bear. How would these stories end? With the truth subsumed by platitudes?

'Certainly this was Gráinne's understanding and this time there would be no poetry and no lament; instead she swore more instant revenge. After allying herself with the forces of her son-in-law Richard 'The Devil's Hook' Bourke, the Bourkes and Uí Mháille rose in rebellion against Bingham's tyranny. Gráinne lived up to her reputation as a fearless and shrewd leader of men in battle and inflicted on the English a number of reverses by way of a violence both savage and stealthy. Thus emboldened she sought a more permanent rejection of English designs, sailing for Ulster to meet with Hugh O'Neill and secure his support of her endeavours.

Now at this point, a fair wind might have seen Gráinne vanquish her most formidable foe. The Spanish King Philip was making preparations for an invasion of Elizabeth's realm in the name of the Church of Rome and Bingham was sent from Connacht to Flanders, to convince the Dutch to side with the English. In his absence Gráinne arranged with the Governor of all Ireland for a pardon for past disloyalties. A short time later, the Spanish set sail in a grand Armada. There were men and ships and cannon from Italy and Portugal and Spain and as England was imperilled so it seemed that Gráinne would soon be free of England's bloodied servants. Alas, there would be no such vanquishing, no such deliverance, no such benign providence, for if Gráinne and the sea were one, then the Spanish enjoyed no comparable relationship. The Armada was dispersed, scattered by unholy winds and towering waves, and many lives were lost around the coasts of Ireland.

Soon after, Bingham – steel and paralysing wind to Gráinne's steel and willow – was sent back to Connacht and tasked by Elizabeth with overseeing the destruction of all who offered comfort to the shipwrecked Spanish sailors. He undertook this villainy with a typical relish, putting to death a thousand hapless Spaniards on the lands of Gráinne and the Devil's Hook alone. In response Gráinne laid waste to the islands of Inishmore, Inishmaan and Inisheer in Galway Bay, to dissuade the English from further encroaching on her territory. But she had been outwitted: whilst she was at sea Bingham despoiled her lands at Carrigahowley and beyond, destroying disparate settlements of kern, confiscating livestock, laying waste to fields of barley. Worse yet, he impounded what remained of Gráinne's fleet and infested the waters of Clew Bay with English galleys and English fighting men.

Bingham's relentless pursuit of Gráinne began to take a terrible toll. Her eyes grew dim and her aspect darkened. For all of her resources she was growing weary of conflict and longed for some respite from English persecution. She turned to her family for sustenance but Bingham had moved to deny her here too with Murchadh bought by twenty English coins and Tibbot na Long placed once more in gaol. And so it was that Gráinne – landless, almost in despair, forced into retreat on land and sea – was visited once more by a profound despair, the like of which she had not known since the death of Donal O'Flaherty.'

The light from the fire has all but died and Maude sits on the bed blank-faced. She grips Gráinne's knife but does not meet

Catherine's gaze. She looks close to tears. This passage of the story is necessarily gruelling and Catherine has to remind herself of her new intent and method, not take too long to drag it back to hope. Perhaps there is a place for platitudes after all?

'For three long days, she eschewed all contact with her kith and, locked away in this very castle, sought refuge in the forest of her mind. There dwelt beasts of course, in thickets of briar – the memories of slanders and slaughter – but she imagined there might also live comfort and, somewhere perhaps, the promise of redemption. And so it was she revisited in reverie all those powerful and jealous men who would have earlier seen her fall, the Joyces of Iarthar Chonnachta, the MacMahons of Ballacroy, the Earl of Desmond, William Thomas and Baron Howth; she recalled her triumphs over rival clans and dark-skinned pirates and English men of war, her alliances with Risdeard an Iarrain, with Sidney, with O'Neill. Was Gráinne's plight to be assuaged by the memory of such previous endeavours? Did these experiences hold lessons on which she might draw?

The answer dearest Maude, is yes, but not in the way she had anticipated. Indeed, the opposite was true. In the depths of her despond, snagged in the entanglements of her past, Gráinne came upon a moment of revelation. She saw that the encounters to which she was paying heed were merely reactions to the world and worse: central to them had been the doings of men. This was not enough. It was not befitting a woman of her stature, a queen among those who would-be kings. As she had grown weary of conflict, so she had also grown weary of the malign intentions of men and weary of the very idea that she should partake of the spoils of their despoiled realm; weary of the idea that she should endure –

and for what? So she could endure again? She would not. She could not. Instead, in her room, Gráinne recalled words that she had spoken, when, after the slaying of her lover Hugh de Lacy, she had vowed her hand would no longer be forced by the hands of others.

'Nothing but the actions of men have brought me low,' she had declared, 'and though I must match them I must also reject their hold on my response.' Instead she would wrest control from fate and despots, and sail again for the open seas of manumission.

I suppose what I am saying here Maude, is that I was wrong to suggest that you should be sanguine in the face of the arrangements that others have made for you. And that you too will come to follow a path more fitting than the one on which you have now embarked, less compromising than the one that has been laid out by self-serving men. As yet I do not know how, for as Gráinne was, you will first be made to flounder in low spirits. But it will happen Maude, you must believe it, you must pin your courage to the sticking place and it will happen to you too.'

Maude is grimly buoyed by these words. She smiles an austere smile, unsheaths Gráinne's knife and holds it aloft, as if in salute. For a moment Catherine supposes it might almost be the rolled-up script of a play, vital and affirming; setting herself against her own tears, she crosses to Maude and puts her hand on the girl's shoulder, before leaving the room.

Friday, Rockfleet Castle

Catherine is exhausted but her heart beats strongly. After the trials and betrayals of the last two days, she is determined: she will not allow any further violations of her spirit, nor Maude's. She will not. Not that this will be easy. She has emerged from the oppression of her thoughts and the walls of Rockfleet into a sea of happenings, a maelstrom. Today is loud, it shrieks and bellows. The castle resounds to violent invective, recrimination. In her room she hears Theobald shouting, then she is angered by the appearance of Patrick and two of Theobald's men. The men carry muskets. Patrick speaks in a flat voice. He doesn't look at Catherine when he addresses her. 'Where is Maude?'

'I do not know. I have not seen her since last night.'

'She has not been with you?'

'I have not seen her since last night.'

'I hope that is the truth. You have been warned about your conduct. You will not be warned again.'

Patrick gestures to the men, who move further into Catherine's room. There is nowhere for anyone to hide and after poking at the covers on her bed, they shake their heads.

'What gives you the right to enter my quarters in this manner?'

Patrick glares. 'Maude is missing. She has not been seen this morning. Nor indeed since she was last with you. John Browne of

79

the Neale is displeased. He does not look well on such disobedience.'

Catherine recalls Maude's state of mind and knows instantly where she will be found. There is rain on the window of her room and she must share the little girl's whereabouts, but she will not speak of this to Patrick. 'Where is Theobald? I have some information to pass on.' Catherine too, speaks without emotion.

Patrick leaves her room. The two soldiers wait. Catherine sees she is to follow Patrick and does. The soldiers bring up the rear. Outside the castle there is much activity once more. By the braziers, a kerfuffle. Half a dozen horses tossing their heads, an angry crush of men; there are voices raised, the sound of steel clacking on steel – was that a gauntlet striking a helmet or something worse? The melee comprises Theobald and the men of the Neale. Theobald addresses a giant man in a felt hat. He is gesticulating wildly. Patrick moves to separate them, brings Theobald to Catherine and Catherine tells Theobald where Maude has gone.

Maude is found sheltering by the side of the track to Kilgeever Abbey. She had a mind to somehow cross to Gráinne's island, and had walked as far as she could in the dark, spent the night against a fallen wall. When she is returned to Rockfleet, Theobald's men return to Catherine's room. 'You will come with us.'

'I don't understand.'

'The girl has been found. She was in possession of a stolen knife.'

'That was my knife. It was a gift to her.'

'It was not yours to give.'

'Am I being arrested? On whose authority?'

'We are returning to Castleburke. We will escort you.'

Catherine is taken outside to a wagon, where she sits with a soldier. Through light rain, she sees the camp outside Rockfleet being taken apart. Tents are pulled down. Cooks and porters load up the wagons, the wagons are hitched to horses. The John Brownes emerge from the castle, followed by Theobald and Patrick; backs are slapped, the earlier animosity forgotten. The families' standards are unfurled and the John Brownes mount up, and ride off. Then Maude appears and is bundled into the coach.

In the back of the wagon, Catherine overhears a conversation between two unseen men. One them is Patrick, the other Conall.

'You will ride on,' says Patrick, 'ahead of us. Arrange for the building of a pillorie.'

'A pillorie? It has been a while. What's the reason?'

'Reason? We have no need of an assizes.'

Conall laughs. Catherine cannot tell if Patrick is joking. 'That will be decided later,' he says. 'An example must be set, that is all.'

In the wagon Catherine shakes her head. She was meant to hear the conversation, she is sure of it. So now she is to be pilloried. Pilloried. Bound and tormented, humiliated and mocked. And for what? Catherine realises she is beyond caring. She has always dammed encroaches on her peace of mind with reason: now reason too has turned its coat. Maude's beating, Patrick's falsity, the speed with which her restive calm has dissipated, has left her dazed. All she can think of is leaving this place. Leaving Mayo, leaving Connacht – leaving Patrick and Theobald – at the earliest opportunity.

The column sets off for Castleburke just before noon. Outside, the sun breaks through for the first time in three days. It is a strong sun too, a life-enhancing mockery of Catherine's desperation. In the back of the wagon, she is thrown about as the soldier sits, impassive. He unwraps some meat and chews. She says 'Can I have some please?' and he waits until it is bone and gristle and throws it to her. The wagon is damp and hot. It steams and smells of musty wet yet Catherine is numb, oblivious to the possible consolations of extant sensation. She returns instead to a place where she is unquestionably alive, where she is a little girl, smelling ink and paper, elated at the sight of the reddest of apples in all the town: this past is fanciful, a benign fiction, soft-hearted and indulgent, a fiction unclouded by pain.

At Castleburke, she is delivered to her cottage at the bottom of the hill. She stumbles from the wagon. It is late afternoon. The sunlight catches the edge of a rain-heavy bulk of slow-moving clouds and lights the canopy of the wood in yellow. Lough Carra glitters beneath a small pool of blue sky. Mayo is beautiful but Catherine is not stirred. At the top of the hill the new house is imperious, overlooking all.

Catherine is startled from a fitful doze by a tapping at the back window of her cottage. She stumbles upright. At the window, lit by the moon, is Maude. The little girl looks serious and her bruises are still pronounced but she breaks into a smile as Catherine blinks the sleep out of her eyes and stares, confused. Maude gestures. Catherine frowns. Maude points and Catherine understands. She crosses to the front door and carefully opens it. Theobald's guard is wrapped up in a blanket, asleep against a tree at the edge of the wood. At his feet a fire smoulders. The moon is bright. Maude comes into view from around the side of the cottage and Catherine ushers her inside. 'What are you doing here?' she whispers.

'I have decided to pin my courage to the sticking place.'

'How did you get here?'

'I know how to escape.'

'But what do you want?'

'I want you to tell me more of Gráinne.'

'I can't. I'm sorry Maude, it's too dangerous.'

'What do you mean? Is it because of the knife? Are you to be punished?'

'We will both get into trouble,' says Catherine. 'The guard. If he wakes…'

'He will not wake. And I want to hear the story. It makes me feel better.'

Catherine's heart aches a little at this. 'How?'

Maude thinks hard. 'I do not know. I cannot say.'

'You do not know? Or you cannot say?'

'Both. It is a good story.'

'I'm afraid I cannot.'

'But why?'

'I have to go. I can't stay here. I have to go somewhere. After I have...'

'...to Dublin? Is it a good place to live?'

Catherine sighs. The girl's face is bright, like a constellation. 'There is a shop selling books. So in some ways it might be.'

'It is better then?'

'That's as much as I can say.'

'Can I come with you?'

'Oh Maude. I'm sorry. You can't. They will look for you and they will find you. As they did today, at the abbey.'

'I have thought about this. We could take a horse.'

Catherine laughs. Shakes her head.

'No, a good horse. One you can ride. We could leave now. Ride through the dark, go to Dublin. They would never find us.'

'We can't,' says Catherine, but there is something in the hopelessness of her situation, something in her feelings towards Maude, something in the girl's insistence. Although a little crazed, she is unquenchable. Catherine blinks herself more fully awake, tries to focus her thoughts, works quickly on an embroidery with threads of many colours.

If she has questioned the value of Gráinne's story, seen its aspect change with each instalment, as the words catch different lights from different flames, the least she can do is finish it. She owes that much; not to Maude perhaps, or even herself, but to Gráinne. But how long has she left? And how plausible is Maude's suggestion?

Could she leave for Dublin tonight, take the girl with her? Theobald is known in the city and there would be no shortage of men who would betray them but her father too is an influential man, with the ear of important men. Life in the city has its privations – it could certainly be injurious to your spirit – but there are diversions. She has just called some of them to mind, said as much. People too. Others with a like perspective or one not dissimilar. So Dublin may present the two of them with something new, the chance to live a little differently. And besides. What is the alternative? What are the alternatives? Catherine smiles. 'You are sure you can take a horse?'

'They are having a party. There is lots of wine. And oat beer.'

'Then what are we waiting for?'

They set off along the road that runs past the cottages at the foot of the hill. The moon is full and there are no clouds. As they edge past Theobald's guard, Catherine holds her breath and Maude avails herself of a bundle from the horse's side. In it, a leg of mutton and a small flask of wine.

Catherine rides the horse, with Maude holding on behind. Maude has been as good as her word and the beast is placid. Catherine cannot navigate at night and the route they take is a matter of faith. She has a mind to keep going until they reach Abha na Sionainne and then to follow it downriver to the ford at Snámh Dá Éan. They ride along the road, with an eye to the woods on either side. They have a few hours at best before their absence is discovered and Catherine is mindful of the need to be within a scramble of a place to hide. As it is, they will have to shelter in daylight hours, maybe even find a roof in a village. If they put enough distance between them and the estate, Catherine is confident she can allay the suspicions they will be sure to arouse. They could just about pass for mother and daughter. They might be displaced, from an English confiscation, or the attentions of a hostile clan. They might be

Royalists. Perhaps she could even tell the truth? No. Not yet. That can wait.

The night is clear and the landscape is lit by the moon. Now they are riding through woods, now next to a hill, black and daunting. They have eaten the mutton and had sips of the wine. The road is not clearly defined. There is no sign of the river, they cannot smell the river, the fresh ancient scent of the river that will take them to a place beyond the woods, beyond the hills, a place in which they will fashion their fortune, a small domain of their own, or so they hope. How far is it? It is impossible to tell. Catherine knows it will be a long journey and she is so very tired. Twice she nearly falls from the horse into sleep. But this doesn't matter. Maude has accepted her injunction to stay quiet and Catherine senses a shared resolve about their passage, a determination if not a clarity of purpose. Even as she is unsure of the direction they are travelling, they must keep going. They must keep going. Catherine looks up at the stars. They dazzle her. She is faint. They will have to stop soon.

Now Maude nearly slips from the horse. Catherine looks back over her shoulder to check on her companion and sees an unsteady line of fire moving quickly along the road they have just travelled. It is torches, carried by men on horseback, this is the only explanation. The fire is getting nearer. Catherine looks about her. On both sides of the road, there is flat land. There is no cover. Catherine rouses herself, forces a smile. 'I should finish the story of Gráinne Ni Mháille,' she says. 'Come. We might just have enough time.' She stops the horse by the side of the road and dismounts, helps a shivering, glazed-eyed Maude from the saddle. The two of them huddle together on wet ground and Catherine glances nervously along the road they have just travelled. They do not have long before they are separated and worse besides.

'And so dear Maude, we have reached the point where Gráinne's spirits were at their lowest, the problems that beset her related not to the trappings of her life but her very survival. In her attempts to fully inhabit the world, she had tried violence and camouflage, diplomacy and wit; now she was forced to resort to that which men had long taken to be their third strong arm, another fathom to their depthless faculty: the bare fact of their sex.

For years it seemed that Gráinne and the English Queen Elizabeth had been wreaking havoc in the thickets of each other's ambition, emerging only to rut like noble stags. They had been, it is undeniable, mortal enemies. But it was also true that they had between them more in common than merely this antipathy. They were each born to lives that were theirs and not, to dreams that gathered and were dispersed like clouds; they were each condemned to be used and discarded, to live in the stories of others who would deny them the contents of their hearts and minds; to live in gibbets, from which their spirit would be free to do naught but disappear. Although they were sworn enemies then, they were of like character too, familiar in a manner that no other could hope to be. And so it was that Gráinne, in possession of the cruellest of the hands that fate might deal, hemmed-in by the forces of a bitter servant and hobbled by the passage of time, found a way once more to overcome her tribulations.

Shortly after Richard Bingham captured Tibbot na Long, Gráinne wrote a letter to Elizabeth. The correspondence was a masterwork. In it she suggested meeting on Elizabeth's land, to discuss her travails and seek some form of clemency. Her tone was politic – she was, after all, a pirate in the eyes of the Crown, and pirates' headless bodies lined the streets of London – but she asked for no pity. Rather she explained the cause of her despair: the imprisonment of her son and the confiscation of her land and property in the name of the English Queen.

The steel running through Gráinne's letter caught Elizabeth's attention. As Gráinne had imagined in Elizabeth, so Elizabeth recognised in Gráinne one of her own kind. Yet the Queen remained cautious; after all, for many moons Gráinne had been mentioned in dispatches by Englishmen who had seen their authority rejected by force or negotiation. Elizabeth wrote back with a nod of her head that was as wary as it was telling. Before any meeting to address the cause of Gráinne's disquiet, she would require of Gráinne that she answer fully eighteen questions, to test the mettle of her fealty. She asked of Gráinne the nature of her ancestor's business, her connections within the clans of Connacht and the circumstances by which she was able to support her family's affairs. By way of reply, Gráinne blamed again her new-found penury on the injustice of the actions Bingham had taken in Elizabeth's name. On the matter of her historical disloyalty, she was careful to respect the delusionary entitlement of Elizabeth and the presumption of the English court and to place it within a context that would be understood. Her supposed villainy, she wrote, was merely the means by which she had tried to secure for her family a future free from the pernicious vicissitudes of clan enmities and tidal shifts in Irish power.

Gráinne's response was enough for Elizabeth and a meeting was arranged. And so it was that Gráinne had found a way once more to break free of the gibbet, to write for herself her own life story. She was now in her sixth decade, yet despite all that she had endured, her star shone more brightly than ever before. The meeting was to take place in Greenwich Castle, on the River Thames; as such Gráinne's story was to end where it had begun, with the tumultuous irrepressible promise of the sea.

She set sail in her finest galley, of supple oak and burnished cannon. enroute to England, she wrote a poem to thank the waters for their providence before clothing herself in the most regal of raiment she possessed, for this was a meeting not between a queen and a subject but between two queens. Indeed, at the moment Gráinne met Elizabeth, she was a hero fit to share the pages with any whose stories we have heard; the equal and more of Meadhbh and Atalanta, of Hippolyta and Boudicca and Beatrice, strong leaders all but none who could surpass her deeds. Except, of course, such comparisons do not tell of the whole story, do not do justice to the consequence of Gráinne's life, for Gráinne was an elemental force, as formidable, inspiring of awe and perilously alluring as the ocean with which she was irrevocably met. Of more importance still, her time in the corporeal realm was not of centuries past but only just over the horizon of these present and benighted days.

About which Maude, I would like to say a few words. Although Bingham was rebuked and censured for his role in Gráinne's persecution, the outcome of Gráinne's meeting with Elizabeth matters less than the fact of its occurrence and all that we may infer from this; what it means for the past as well as what might come. The point is, dearest Maude, that whatever fate may leave in your path, whichever roads God leads you along, you must remember that such a realm – of feminine strength and influence, of feminine dominion and command – existed and may yet again. But that also, if it is to, we are to make it, or at least try.'

And with that Catherine wraps her arms around Maude and kisses the top of the little girl's head. Maude smiles, weakly but with determination. Catherine hears hoofbeats, horses snorting and men

88

shouting – Patrick, Conall – and as their pursuers are upon them, she raises her face and stares defiantly beyond the flames of the torches, into the dark.

Extract from The Two Queens (continued)

ELIZABETH:
[Pours wine]
So. Where were we? Oh yes. More wine?

GRACE:
Thank you. Although if it pleases you, I would like to get to the heart of my entreaty without further ado.

ELIZABETH:
As you wish.

GRACE:
Thank you. As Your Majesty has already implied, I have come here as both a conscientious subject and as Chieftain of the Clan O'Malley. And - as Your Majesty is also aware - I have come to ask for your

assistance in managing the attentions of Your Majesty's deputies.

ELIZABETH:
I see.

GRACE:
Most particularly Sir Richard Bingham, Your Majesty's Governor in the West of Ireland. It is my contention that his behaviour is not fitting of a servant of the Queen of England. And is, in fact, closer to that of a brigand, a savage-

ELIZABETH:
[Angrily]
-Let me stop you there. A brigand? A savage? Honesty is one thing but there are matters of etiquette of which it would pay to be aware. Richard Bingham is a Knight of the Realm. If you would speak of him I would suggest you choose your words more carefully.

GRACE:
With respect I can assure Your Majesty that - in this instance - I chose my words with the utmost care.

ELIZABETH:
[Musing]
You did?

GRACE:
I did.

ELIZABETH:
Oh yes, I see. Very good. Please continue.

GRACE:
Thank you. Bingham pits one clan against another. He has no respect for property or possessions. More importantly, his disdain for Irish law and the people of Connaught risks turning the whole of Ireland against the rule of Your Majesty. And as Your Majesty has spent much of her reign investing in the loyalty of the Irish people-

ELIZABETH:
-I have?

GRACE:
I believe you know the policy as Submit and Regrant? An arrangement by which you bestow titles on those who give up their land to the Crown-

ELIZABETH:
-Oh that. Yes. Loyalty. I see-

GRACE:
-Indeed. And it would seem wise to protect such an investment. And whilst there are many who might

claim to be able to offer that protection, I would suggest that I am uniquely placed to do so. What I am therefore asking of Your Majesty is that you provide me with assistance in this cause-

ELIZABETH:
[Amazed, looking on Grace]
-Surely you have not come to ask for gold?

GRACE:
[Looking on Elizabeth]
No, I would not dream of asking for gold. Rather that you provide me with the written authority to use whatever means necessary to oppose the actions of all those who would undermine your power.

ELIZABETH:
[Musing a little]
I see. So you would fight my Irish wars?

GRACE:
If Your Majesty wishes to put it like that.

ELIZABETH:
I would. I also note again your choice of words. You said 'All those who would undermine my power' but did not repeat the name of Bingham-

GRACE:
-Your Majesty is most observant-

ELIZABETH:
-I am. And as a consequence of that, I am going to stop you again, in order that I may be spared any more of this deception.

GRACE:
I'm not sure I follow.

ELIZABETH:
[Sighs]
Oh come now. You may be wearing a commoner's dress but you are a queen, of sorts at least-

GRACE:
-You're too kind. And that is at issue here?

ELIZABETH:
[Stands]
On the contrary. You have a thousand head of cattle, a score of castles to your name. This very afternoon you have shown yourself undizzied by ermine and gold-

GRACE:
[Stands]
-I would certainly hope so-

ELIZABETH:
-You have the respect of many men-

GRACE:
-The fear of many men-

ELIZABETH:
-The ear of many men-

GRACE:
-They are perhaps the same.

ELIZABETH walks over to the fire, muses, turns back to Grace

ELIZABETH:
[Earnestly]
Indeed. The point is that you have proved yourself a Leader of men. And as such, I would expect you to speak as one. When I warned you to choose your words with care, I did not mean for you to try to convince me of your cause by talking with such a tortuously judicious tongue. We are drinking wine. Enjoy it. Let it give wings to your speech.

GRACE:
As you imply, Your Majesty, I am no stranger to giving voice to my concerns in the manner you describe. Nor, as it happens, am I unused to drinking wine, even if I am more familiar with oat beer. However, and with respect, I am here today because Your Majesty's servants are exercising Your

Majesty's authority in a manner against which - despite all of my resources - I am helpless. As such, I considered it politic to address you in a manner that might be considered diplomatic.

ELIZABETH:
[Animated]
Nonsense. You and I both know that politics and diplomacy are the cups and balls of foolish men, of interest only to those deluded skulkers who see in them a reason to be. Many men have tried to outwit me with politics and diplomacy and I have seen through them all. Yet it seems as though you have learned at their feet.

GRACE:
I have done no such thing. I do not care for the feet of men. Nor any part besides.

ELIZABETH:
That is not what I have heard. What of Donal O' Flaherty? Hugh de Lacey? Richard in Iron?

GRACE:
[Turning from Elizabeth, softly]
Your Majesty is well informed. Though I am not sure I have learned much from any Irish man save of the many shades of belligerence.

ELIZABETH:

Ha! Very good! I am right in saying though, am I not, that it isn't politics that has cemented your position as a leader of men, nor diplomacy that has brought you to my court.

GRACE:

Your Majesty?

ELIZABETH:

You have sailed ships, fought Barbary pirates. I have heard many tales of thievery at sea.

GRACE:

[Boldly]

It is true that men at your command have trailed riches in the ocean. And I have dipped into them from time-to-time.

ELIZABETH:

My point exactly! And therein lies your power. You are a woman of peculiar qualities. A refusal to yield. A strength of will. We are like rivers, you and I, forces of nature. This is what has brought you here today and this is what I may choose to reward with my favour. So. Take it upon my word: be true to yourself, for it is has got you where you are.

GRACE:
[Walking around the room, musing]
It would seem I am to be warned off speaking in one manner and damned for trying another.

ELIZABETH:
Maybe so. Maybe that is the lot of those who would parley with me when I am tired of being parleyed with.

GRACE:
[Boldly]
That is your prerogative. And I appreciate the generous way you choose to exercise your power, by sharing advice in such a bountiful manner.
However. I am not sure that your comments amount to quite the compliment you may have intended them to be. Is it possible, Your Majesty, that you have spent too long in the company of your own deluded skulkers?

ELIZABETH:
Now it is I who am confused.

GRACE:
And I who find that hard to believe. You say that we are forces of nature, and I have heard this said before. But such a description diminishes us.

ELIZABETH:

How?

GRACE:

[Pacing, musing]

If we are judged by what is natural we are contained, entrapped by it too. We may be forces of nature, but we are also women who have broken nature's laws: I am a Pirate Queen, and you are an Heirless Queen; I am Grainne the Bald and you are Elizabeth, cussed, aloof-

ELIZABETH:

Be careful now. I would refer you to my earlier warning-

GRACE:

[Turns to look fixedly on Elizabeth]

-I am only speaking the truth! Where is my love of poetry in such a description? Where is your evident liking for an afternoon goblet of wine? For making the acquaintance of a one-time enemy of your realm? No, I may be a pirate but I would rather be judged by my navigation of our complicated world than by my willingness - or otherwise - to conform to the laws of nature, by which some would have us believe it is governed.

ELIZABETH:

[Amazed]

Can this be? Grace O'Malley, misunderstood? The Sea Queen of Connaught a precious flower? Surely such objections are a waste of time. Are we not what others make of us?

GRACE:

Of course! But we must fight against their invocations, even as they encase us. Otherwise we risk becoming the person we are held to be, constrained as if by gibbets.

ELIZABETH:

[Turning from her, musing a little]

Perhaps. But then I am not sure I care. I am an old woman. As a river I have nearly reached the sea. I have to pick my diversions with care.

GRACE:

Oh I too, Your Majesty, I can assure you of that.

ELIZABETH:

Besides. Who we are is not for us to decide. We do not become whole in life but death. And it is by history that we will be defined.

GRACE:
If at all. With respect, this may be why you do not care about your reputation as it now stands.

ELIZABETH:
Pray tell?

GRACE:
Because your history is assured! For it is written in the language of power and power records its own! Whereas my life will disappear if I do not write it in my blood, as I live it. If it is left to mere projection and myth to give it shape.

ELIZABETH:
[Musing, looking fixedly on Grace]
Your words are bitter. Is this you and I of whom you speak? Or your country and mine?

GRACE:
[Softly, an aside]
Whichever Your Majesty wishes.

ELIZABETH:
[Happily]
Very good. Here Grace O'Malley, have the last of this wine with me. I have to say this afternoon has made for me the change I hoped it might.

You have demonstrated the gift of - oh how should I put this? - a most eloquent tongue. You'll stay awhile? Take some food? I'll wager you have some stories you'd like to share.

GRACE:
Your Majesty is most kind. But I have occupied enough of your valuable time.

ELIZABETH:
Oh. A pity.
[Pauses]
A pity.

GRACE:
Indeed. And as to the business of the day?

ELIZABETH:
Yes, of course. On that I have to say I am not convinced of the rightness of your cause.
[Pauses]
And yet it is clear that we are divided by less than joins us together. You shall have your alliance and your authority. But before you go, I would like to propose a toast.

GRACE:
[Smiling]
Thank you Ma'am. To Ireland?

ELIZABETH:
Ha! I think not.

GRACE:
The Irish then?

ELIZABETH:
Your wit is dry. No, I had in mind something altogether more civilised. Shall we drink to history? And to queens?

GRACE:
[Turning from Elizabeth, softly]
To queens.

Friday 1st October, 1660 – Westport, County Mayo

The house at Westport looks like many Catherine has seen on her trip across the ravaged country. There is grey stone, there are neat hedges, beds of roses. It is a halfway house: now a castle – buttressed against ghosts, with violence in its stone – now a place of recreation and repose – open to the possibility of a less haunted future – if already weathered by cold rain. Catherine dismounts. There is a young woman sitting on a seat overlooking the lake and Catherine is pleased to see that she is on her own; she is anxious and has no desire to speak to anyone else.

Catherine approaches Maude, who looks up. Recognition is instant but Catherine cannot tell what comes next in Maude's eyes. Maude holds her gaze. 'It has been a while.'

'It has.'

Maude pauses. Remembers herself, who she is. She looks away. 'Why are you here?'

'I have brought you a gift. An indulgence of mine. A piece of writing I thought you might like to see.'

On her return to Dublin, Catherine continued to teach and query, herself and others. The city was awash with intrigue and duplicity, with recrimination and a new-found solidarity and at first she swirled happily enough in its eddies. Then she tired of their relentlessness. Her real interest, she decided, lay in enthusing men of letters about the story of the Pirate Queen and so she wrote a play. She wrote with her experience of Mayo on her mind and eventually, as the years passed and she tried in vain to find an audience for her work, she decided that Maude herself would be a more receptive reader.

Maude does not engage with her. 'Is it Patrick?' she says. 'Have you come to see Patrick?'

'Patrick is still alive?'

'He is.'

'I see. But no.'

'He saved your life. That night. Talked my father out of…'

Catherine frowns. 'Maybe. But that is not how I remember him.' She hasn't thought of Patrick at all on her journey, but now she hears his name, she is moved; by what, she neither knows nor dwells on. Will she mention her script again? She is unsure. She gestures towards the big house, the lake. 'Is all this yours?'

'Now my father is dead,' says Maude.

'I heard. It was news in Dublin. I am sorry.'

'There is no need.'

Theobald was shot for his part in the events at Shrule and although Catherine is sorry, this is not why she is here either. She sighs. It has been a long journey and she is beginning to think it might, in part at least, have been wasted. She had imagined a more welcoming Maude but now it feels like a long decade since she left, almost twenty years in ten. For all that the people of Mayo and the people of Dublin are more closely entwined than ever before – fused by English fire – it is as though her life and that of her one-time charge and confidante have diverged in such a way as to leave an unbridgeable gap between them. 'You are content then? I mean your life is good?'

'My husband is a good man.'

'This is no small thing. These are dangerous times for a woman to be alone.'

'They are,' says Maude, but Catherine sees in her aspect something close to doubt, an opportunity perhaps.

'Do you remember? When you were a little girl? Content was not enough – '

'Please don't. I cannot.'

'– you were wilful. Determined – '

'I cannot.'

'– enthralled by what I told you of Gráinne Ni Mháille. Do you still have her knife?'

'I do.'

'Well then! I am going to Clare Island and I wondered if – '

'I cannot.'

'– no?'

'I'm sorry,' says Maude.

Catherine bows her head then nods, defeated but undefeated, resigned but determined still. It is clear the moment has passed, long ago. Maude has little interest in Gráinne, still less in Catherine's writing and Catherine has erred in imagining she would have. It is no matter. There are doubtless reasons – there are always reasons – but they will not deter her. Instead she must keep going. She must keep going. She and Maude embrace and she mounts up and rides off towards the coast, towards Kilgeever Abbey and Clare Island, towards Gráinne and the sea.

Cast of characters: 1530 - 1603

Gráinne Ni Mháille. Also known as: Grace O'Malley; Gráinne Mhaol; the Dark Lady of Doona; the Pirate Queen. Clan chief and pirate. Born 1530, died 1603.

Dónal 'an Chogaidh' Ó Flaithbheartaigh. Also known as Donal of the Battles. First Husband of Gráinne Ni Mháille. Died 1565.

Risdeard 'an Iarainn' Bourke. Also known as Richard in Iron. Second husband of Gráinne Ni Mháille. Died 1583.

Tibbot 'na Long' Bourke. 1st Viscount Mayo. Irish parliamentarian. Son of Gráinne Ni Mháille and Risdeard 'an Iarainn' Bourke. Born 1567, died 1629.

Sir Henry Sidney. Lord Deputy of Ireland. Born 1529, died 1586.

Sir Richard Bingham. English soldier and naval commander. Governor of Connacht. Born 1528, died 1599.

Cast of characters: 1650 - 1660

Maude Bourke. Great great granddaughter of Gráinne Ni Mháille, daughter of Theobald Bourke. Born 1640. Married to Colonel John Browne, 1654.

Theobald Bourke. Third Viscount Mayo. Great Grandson of Gráinne Ni Mháille. Executed by the English in 1652.

Colonel John Browne. Husband of Maude Bourke. Born 1631, died 1711.

John Browne. 1st Baronet Browne of the Neale. Father of Colonel John Browne. Born 1604, died 1670.

Note for readers

I can't remember when I first heard of Gráinne Ni Mháille. I've a feeling I saw a picture on Facebook, of a statue in Westport, County Mayo, but when and why, I couldn't say. What I do know is that after the merest of reading around her life, I found her story irresistible.

For a figure of such historical significance, surprisingly little has been written about Gráinne's life. As of 2022 there have been a couple of biographies (another, from historian Gillian Kenny, is forthcoming), a handful of novelisations, and a musical which ran for 8 months, in 2006/2007. And that's it. This piqued my interest. Was Gráinne nearly written out of history because of the systematic English suppression of indigenous Irish culture? Was Ireland's tradition of oral storytelling a contributory factor? Or was her absence in the written record a reflection of male power, and the position of women in pre-modern Ireland?

I decided then, that the novel wasn't just going to be a fictionalisation of the major events of Gráinne's life. Instead I wanted to place her story into this context, to ask questions of her treatment, to ask if stories can be owned, or reclaimed, and if so, how and by whom. To do this, I had to acknowledge my own role in some of the processes that feed into these questions.

This acknowledgement starts with the novel's relationship to the objective truth. Which is, as with all historical fiction, both complex and compromised. For instance, depending on your source, Sir Henry Sidney was either someone who: 'cautiously implemented Queen Elizabeth I's policy of imposing English laws and customs on the Irish' (Encyclopedia Britannica), or the person responsible for the massacre at Mullaghmast in 1577, part of a 'pattern of conquest which implicated not only the soldiers and settlers who served in the Gaelic localities, but also the upper echelons of the English administration in Ireland' (Irish Historical Studies, 1999).

Then there are events that have passed into myth. For example, although there was an exchange of correspondence between Gráinne and Elizabeth 1st, in which Elizabeth asked Gráinne to prove her loyalty to the Crown of England, it is unlikely that the two ever met. Similarly, it is generally accepted that Gráinne's son, Tibbot Bourke, was born at sea (hence 'na long', or 'of the ships'); what is less certain is the veracity of the version of the story that has Gráinne, minutes after giving birth, repelling an attack from Barbary pirates, with Tibbot in her arms.

There are also characters that are purely my invention (Catherine and Patrick didn't actually live), and those with whom I've taken liberties: Maude Bourke was married at 14, but although it is more than possible, there is no evidence she met her future husband at the age of 10.

Despite this, there is information in the novel that is verifiably accurate. Few would argue with the following appraisal of Sir Richard Bingham, from The English Historical Review (2008): 'Every Court in Ireland, every tested servant of the Crown, every grandee looking for encouragement to engage with Crown administration, indeed the Crown administration itself, could not be confident of prevailing of Bingham, whose conscience – insofar as he had any – was merely the lawyer to his will, and whose powerful protector was willing to enforce that will. Mutual respect between the Crown and the majority of its Irish subjects – already far advanced – became ever more entrenched as a result.'

Catherine's version of Gráinne's story is a mixture of all of these elements. And omissions too. The stuff I've left out. This is unavoidable: providing context is one thing, but there has to be a focus. And all I can do is hope the one I've chosen does the story of The Pirate Queen some justice.

Acknowledgements

With thanks to Rose and Alan at Stairwell Books, Edinburgh University for the image of Gráinne meeting Elizabeth;. Andrea for the usual; Gillian Kenny and Ruth Gilligan for their time and generosity.

.

Other books for young people available from Stairwell Books

Key Stage 3 / Young Adult

Shadow Cat Summer	Rebecca Smith
The Water Bailiff's Daughter	Yvonne Hendrie
The Return of the Mantra: Blood Gift Chronicles Book 1	Susie Williamson
The Warder: Blood Gift Chronicles Book 2	Susie Williamson

Key Stage 1-2

Harriet The Elephotamus	Fiona Kirkman
A Business of Ferrets	Alwyn Bathan
Very Bad Gnus	Suzanne Sheran
Season of the Mammoth	Antony Wootten
The Grubby Feather Gang	Antony Wootten
Mouse Pirate	Dawn Treacher
Rosie and John's Magical Adventure	The Children of Ryedale District Primary Schools

For further information please contact rose@stairwellbooks.com

www.stairwellbooks.co.uk
@stairwellbooks

Lightning Source UK Ltd.
Milton Keynes UK
UKHW012306111022
410341UK00002B/108